ESPECIALLY FOR GIRLS™ *presents*

Karen and Vicki

ELISABET McHUGH

GREENWILLOW BOOKS • New·York

Library of Congress Cataloging in Publication Data

McHugh, Elisabet.
Karen and Vicki.
Summary: When Karen's mother marries, Karen
must learn to adapt to living with a complete
family, and in particular with her older
step-sister, Vicki. Sequel to "Karen's Sister."
[1. Stepchildren—Fiction.
2. Family life—Fiction] I. Title.
PZ7.M47863Kap 1984   [Fic]   83-14156
ISBN 0-688-02543-9

Chapter 1

This morning, for the first time in history, I was late for school. I'm in a special class for gifted students, and our room is in the basement; that means every morning I have to battle all the high school kids that are going downstairs for PE. And believe me, that's no picnic. Once somebody shoved an elbow in my face and gave me a black eye.

When I opened the door to the classroom, Mr. Campbell turned around. He raised his eyebrows; but he didn't say anything, and anyway, I was only a few minutes late.

Later, when he came over to check my work, he said, "Well, Karen, have you thought about what kind of special project you would like to do?" He sat down on the empty desk beside me and folded his arms.

Up until that moment I hadn't, but right then I got this

brilliant idea. "I'd like to work on getting my family more organized," I said.

He raised his eyebrows again. "I see," he said after a moment. "Any particular reason why?"

"Yeah," I said bitterly. "I was late today because Vicki locked herself in the bathroom for almost twenty minutes. And all she did was play around with her hair."

Mr. Campbell tapped his cheek with the ruler and stared into space. After a while he focused his eyes on me again. "You know, that's not a bad idea." He nodded his head and repeated, "Not bad at all."

After a moment he added, "Let me think about it for a while."

I hoped he'd let me do it because the project would take the place of regular homework. I'm in the seventh grade this year, but I've been doing mostly eighth-grade work, which isn't too bad; still, sometimes even that gets boring.

After lunch Mr. Campbell said I could go ahead. The project will be called TES, which is short for Time Efficiency Study. He told me to get a notebook because I have to keep a journal for the next few weeks. I'm supposed to write down how much time different family members spend on doing things at home, and then I have to figure out ways for them to use their time more efficiently.

Mr. Campbell said it might be a good idea to check with my family before I started, just in case they had some objections.

When I told Mom about it, she said it sounded interesting, and wouldn't it be great if I could get Vicki to clean up the mess in her room once in a while instead of spending all her time reading romance books? I said I'd do my best, but she'd better not expect any miracles.

Vicki, who is sixteen, hasn't cleaned her room since she moved into it.

Dad wished me good luck and promised me ten dollars if I could get the boys to stop playing their electronic games. The beep-beep is driving him up the wall.

My brother Ryan, who is six, pointed out that if I'm going to time everything, then maybe I can prove that he gets to watch less TV than anybody else.

Meghan offered to help with my project, and I told her I could use all the help I can get. Meghan is three weeks younger than Ryan, and she is Korean and adopted like me.

Marcus, who is fourteen, said I'd better not write anything personal in my journal or he'd break my neck. Marcus has been trying to kiss Susie Nelson, and I guess that's what he is worried about.

Vicki said she couldn't care less about my project, and I'd better not bug her with it.

Grandma, who is living with us, said she didn't think it would work. It was too late for us to change. Now, if we had been brought up properly in the first place . . .

I didn't stop to listen to the rest of her speech since I'd heard it a hundred times already.

Mom offered to lend me her stopwatch. She uses it when she goes jogging, as she does every morning, except, of course, the last couple of months. She is going to have a baby soon.

I hope the baby will be a girl. So does Meghan; but she wants Mom to give *her* the baby to keep, and then Meghan will give Mom all her dolls instead.

Ryan wants a brother, and if it turns out to be a girl, he wants Mom to trade it in for a hamster. Marcus is worried that he'll have to baby-sit, which would be embarrassing, and Vicki doesn't care whether it's a boy or a girl as long as Mom hurries up and has it so she can get back to normal. Vicki has to help around the house a lot more now because of Mom's pregnancy.

Grandma hasn't made up her mind yet what the baby is going to be. She believes a lot in premonition. "Premonition" was one of my new words last year. It means forewarning, like when you know something before it actually happens. I'm supposed to learn at least ten new words each week, and I can pick any words I want from the dictionary.

Anyway, Grandma goes to sales a lot, and when she found five skeins of baby blue yarn for only two dollars just when she was going to knit something for the baby, she said it was a sure sign Mom was going to have a boy. That lasted for about a month until she saw the cutest pink and white baby dress at the mall for less than half price. Then she said Fate had brought her there. She bought the dress, and after that she referred to the baby as "she." *That* lasted until she found Ryan's old baby clothes in the attic when she was looking for a photo album. Now she isn't sure what it's going to be, and in the meantime, she calls the baby "it."

I knew, of course, that ours was a pretty easygoing household, but I didn't realize how bad it was until I started my TES. I guess living in the middle of something makes you blind to a lot of things.

For the record I want to tell you that I'm not at all like the rest of the family. I like things to be neat and orderly. I never have to clean my room because it's never messy. When I change my clothes, I always put them where they belong, and everything has its special place.

This summer, when I told Mom that I had memorized where my clothes were hanging in the closet, so I could take out everything I wanted with my eyes closed, she said, "What if you hang something in the wrong place?"

I gave her a pitying look. "But I never do. I always put everything where it's supposed to be."

Mom raised her eyes to the ceiling and said, "I don't believe it. I just don't believe it."

"Come, I'll show you," I offered.

But Mom only shook her head and mumbled, "I wonder where I went wrong,"—whatever that meant.

When I asked her if she'd rather have me live in a dump like Vicki, she sighed and said that sometimes she wasn't sure.

I didn't think that was funny.

"You should be grateful that at least one person in the family wears clothes that match," I said.

"Oh, I am," Mom said fervently.

My mother is tall and blond and very pretty, and she dresses beautifully when she really puts her mind to it; but she isn't interested in clothes the way I am.

I mean, if she wants to wear her green slacks and she finds out that the top that goes with it is in the laundry, then she gets another top that kind of matches but really isn't the right thing. And it doesn't bother her.

I used to take care of Mom's clothes, too, but that was before we married into this family. Now everything is different. Sometimes I have trouble remembering how things used to be, even though it wasn't that long ago.

Chapter 2

I'm twelve and a half now, and when I was almost eleven and a half, Mom and I were still living all by ourselves.

Mom was single then, and we had an old farmhouse a couple of miles away from where we live now. Mom is a veterinarian, and she has an animal clinic in town. .

Anyway, she adopted me from Korea when I was only four, and I have taken care of her practically ever since. She always wanted to have children, but she wasn't ready to get married yet. Then last year Mom thought it was time to add another member to our family, and that's when we got Meghan.

We were on our way from the airport after picking Meghan up when we had a flat tire. It was one o'clock in the morning, and we all were tired, and Meghan was still sick from having been on the plane all the way from Korea. We hadn't seen another car on the highway for at least an hour, and I remember Mom groaning when she discovered that she didn't even have a flashlight. How was she going to change the tire in the dark?

Pretty soon Meghan and Mom's mother, who was with us, went to sleep in the car, and Mom and I stood outside, ready to wave down any car that might come along. I guess we were lucky because it was only a couple of minutes later that this pickup stopped and a man offered to help. That's how Mom met Dad.

They got married three months later, and Mom and I and Meghan moved in with Dad and his kids and their grandmother. Mom leased out our house until she could decide whether to sell it or not.

Dad's name is John Carlson, and ever since his first wife died, which was three years ago, Vicki and Marcus and Ryan's grandmother had taken care of them.

After Mom and Dad were married, Grandma said she was moving, but Mom talked her out of that. Grandma has a small apartment over the garage, which is separate from the house.

I don't know what we would have done without Grandma. My mother might be a good vet, but she is really hopeless when it comes to running a house. Before she married, *I* was the one who took care of things.

Mom is still working at the clinic, except, of course, for the last six weeks. She was getting too heavy to be able to be on her feet all day, and she couldn't go out on farm calls any more. And more than half the work involves farm animals.

Dad is a science professor at the university, and even though he is pretty busy with his work, which is research, he is always there when I need someone to talk to. He is really neat, and it's nice to have a father like everybody else.

Right before Meghan came, I tried really hard to marry off my mother, but Mom wasn't at all interested in finding a husband. By the time my sister arrived I had given up, and when she told me four weeks later that she was going to marry this man who had three kids of his own, I almost died.

Like I said, that was a year ago, and a lot has happened since then. We've all gotten used to living together, although it hasn't always been easy. For months Mom said she felt she was running a restaurant. She wasn't used to having to cook for so many. And of course, both she and I had trouble getting used to standing in line for the bathroom. There is only one bathroom in this house.

Meghan is the only who has adjusted most easily. But then, of course, she is the youngest, and she really can't remember living any other way.

I asked Grandma once what she thought about the whole thing, and she said she was glad Dad finally decided to remarry. After the wedding she asked us to call her Grandma, like the other kids did. I thought it was nice that she didn't mind getting two more grandchildren all of a sudden.

Grandma is seventy-six. She has been living in the apartment over the garage since her husband died six years ago. Before that she lived in Seattle.

In the beginning this house seemed pretty big; but now it isn't big enough, and it's difficult to have some peace and quiet.

Next spring we are moving to our old house. Somebody is renting it now; but Dad has talked to a contractor, and in March they will start building a new wing, which will make it large enough for all of us. It's much nicer out there anyway because it's up on a hill with a view, while this is boxed in between two patches of woods.

I can't wait to move back to the farm because I miss the pond and the barn and everything else. My horse is still out there, too, and Gordon is taking care of it. Gordon is a logger who lives nearby, and he used to help Mom with a lot of things when we lived at our old place.

The addition will be on the east side of the house, and it will have four bedrooms, two baths, and a family room. I'll get my old room back then.

Tomorrow is Friday. I've decided to use the first week of my TES to time everybody and find out what needs to be changed. After that I'll start worrying about what to do to help them.

I won't concentrate too much on Mom since she is pregnant and all that. Besides, before we came into this family, I tried for years to get her more organized, and it never worked anyway.

It might take me awhile to straighten everybody out, especially Vicki, but I know that once I'm through, they will be grateful to me forever after.

Chapter 3

When I came home from school today, everybody else was already home. That's because I had a piano lesson right after class. Mom was lying down because her back was hurting, and Grandma was in the kitchen, fixing dinner.

"Is that you, Karen?" she called as I was walking up the stairs. "Could you ask your mother if she wants me to make a salad?"

I went into Mom's room. She was reading a book. I walked over and gave her a kiss. "How was your piano lesson?" she asked.

"Okay. Grandma wants to know if we are having salad."

"I don't think so. Tell her there is some cake left in the other refrigerator that we can have for dessert."

Mom is really getting big. The baby is due in about three weeks. I think it will be kind of exciting to have a baby in the house, except for one thing: I have to move in with Vicki.

When Mom first told me a month ago, I said incredulously, "You mean I have to live in that pigpen?"

"It isn't all that bad," Mom said unconvincingly.

"It's not fair," I muttered, but Mom pretended not to hear.

I don't intend to move in with Vicki until Mom goes to the hospital. All that needs to be moved anyway is my bed and dresser and my bookcase. I hope my TES project will make Vicki shape up before then, but I don't have much faith it will.

I can't wait until we move back to the other house. I might not live that long, of course. One winter with Vicki could kill anybody.

I went down to the kitchen and told Grandma about the cake. Then I opened my notebook. "What time did you start dinner?" I asked.

"Oh," Grandma said vaguely, "maybe half an hour ago." She opened the oven door to check the potatoes.

"And when do you think it will be ready?"

She wiped her hands on the apron and started filling the sink with hot water. "In another twenty minutes or so. But we're not eating until your father comes home."

I already knew that. Dad usually comes home at five-thirty. Now it was four-thirty, meaning that dinner would be ready ten minutes to five and would have to be kept warm for at least forty minutes until we were ready to eat.

I explained that to Grandma and suggested it might be better if she'd start cooking a little later. That would give her more free time.

"Oh, I don't mind," she said. "I wasn't doing anything anyway."

I sighed. "That's not the point," I explained patiently. "I just thought maybe you could find something constructive to do with your time."

Grandma stared at me over her glasses. "Is that so?" she said tartly. "Like what, if I may ask?"

I chewed on my pen and tried to think of something. "Janet's grandmother goes to exercise classes," I said finally.

Grandma's mouth fell open. "Goodness gracious!" she exclaimed. "Well, I guess if she wants to make a fool of herself, that's her business." She scrubbed the pot vigorously with a soap pad. "As far as I'm concerned, I'm thankful if I can bend over far enough to put my shoes on in the morning."

I've decided to exclude Grandma from my project. That means she won't be in it. "Exclude" is one of the words I learned last month.

Mom said once that when people get old, they get very set in their ways, and I guess that's what happened to Grandma.

It was Marcus's turn to do the dishes and Ryan's turn to dry. That took them almost an hour and a half because they spent a lot of time hitting each other with the wet dishtowels and arguing about a pot that Ryan said wasn't clean and Marcus said it was, too.

Vicki was on the phone for forty-five minutes, talking to Debbie, and then she stood in front of the hall mirror for another ten minutes, examining a pimple she had on her forehead.

When I asked her if she was done with her homework, she said it was none of my business, and why didn't I crawl under the kitchen sink and die? She says things like that all the time; that shows you what kind of person she is. I tell you, sharing a room with her will be a riot.

Vicki is a junior this year, and all she ever thinks about is boys, boys, boys. The only ones she goes out with, however, are deadbeats like Harry Jenkins, who has bad breath, and Elroy Symms, who is much shorter than she is. But since she acts the same way at school as she does at home, it's a miracle that she has any dates at all.

She is always experimenting with her hair and her face, and believe me, sometimes it's pretty embarrassing to have her around. Mom won't let Vicki wear makeup unless she puts it on tastefully, but Vicki goes to the bathroom at school and smears on lots more before the first period. Then she washes it off before she goes home.

Friday is the day we're supposed to clean our rooms. That means everybody but me. Mine is never messy, so all I do is vacuum.

Marcus and Ryan are sharing a room, and their idea of cleaning is to stuff everything in the drawers and under the beds. When Gradma checks on them, they usually have to start over, but Mom only opens the door and looks around and says it looks pretty good.

Today Mom was up and around after dinner, so the boys got away with it again. Vicki always says she'll clean her room as soon as she is done with her homework; that's the same as never since her homework never gets done. If I had grades like hers, I'd kill myself, but Vicki doesn't seem to mind as long as she isn't actually flunking.

Just before dark I took a walk with the dogs. It was down the road and back again since Arthur isn't very big on walks. Arthur is our sheepdog, and he tries so hard not to be a bother that he really is a nuisance. He has a tendency to get overweight, so I try to make him take at least one short walk every day; but no matter how slowly I walk, he falls behind, and I practically have to drag him home.

Arthur's coat has this strange pinkish color, which is why he has such an inferiority complex. Most of the time he looks as if he wished the floor would open up and swallow him. It's really sad. My other dog is Lord Nelson, who is a very ordinary dog, but he has only one eye. He and I have a lot of fun together, and he is very well mannered, and you hardly ever know he's around. Arthur, on the other hand, is always in the way, and everybody runs into him or trips over him, making him feel even worse.

At night Arthur sleeps by my bed and Lord Nelson on top of it. Sometimes it's hard for me to get any rest because Arthur snores terribly. For a while I tried to get him to move in with Mom and Dad instead since Arthur used to sleep in Mom's room before we came here. That lasted only one night. Arthur didn't sleep at all. He just stood by the bed staring at Dad the whole night. Dad said it was the most horrible experience he had ever had. He could feel Arthur's eyes on him the whole time, and every time he turned on the light Arthur's big, hairy head was just a few inches away.

Dad said it wouldn't have been so bad if he could only see his eyes; but of course, Arthur's hair hangs over his face, and you can't see his eyes at all. Mom thought it was really funny. She explained to Dad that Arthur was just waiting for him to go away. Then Dad said that she'd better explain to Arthur that things had changed, but Mom said that poor Arthur's brain was too overloaded with new things already.

Saturday I got up early so I could work on my project.

Everybody has to fix his own breakfast, and since I was the first one up, I scrambled two eggs and made some toast. Then I watched cartoons until eight, when Ryan showed up. He took his cereal into the family room so he could watch TV while he was eating. When he was done, there were cornflakes all over the carpet.

Grandma soft-boiled one egg and made a cheese sandwich, and since Meghan came into the kitchen while she was doing that, she boiled another egg for her. Meghan is Grandma's favorite.

Dad made French toast for himself and Mom. Marcus spilled more cereal on the carpet. Breakfast lasted from seven until ten-thirty, and in the end the kitchen counter and the stove were covered with stacks of dirty dishes.

Vicki was still sleeping, and anyway, she never eats breakfast if she can avoid it. Most of the time she is on a diet.

Grandma had to wash all the dishes and clean up the kitchen so she'd have room to make lunch. It's obvious that if anything ever needs to be reorganized in this house, it's Saturday morning breakfast.

After I had vacuumed the living room, which took me exactly seven minutes, I went over to the Reddingers'. Jenny Reddinger is my best friend. I hadn't seen her for two days because she had been home with the flu. Today her mother said I could come in because Jenny was much better. The Reddingers live down the road from us.

Mom was up and around all evening, and I followed her with my stopwatch. She made three trips to the basement with laundry, and then she walked from room to room, looking for something. When I asked her what she was looking for, she said she couldn't remember, but she'd know as soon as she found it. She never did, however, and after a while she decided to take a walk. It took her twelve minutes to find her sneakers. They were under a chair in the living room.

Sunday morning, when everybody should have been ready for church, both Marcus and Ryan suddenly had to go the bathroom. Vicki was already in there, of course, so first we had to wait for her, and then we had to wait for the boys. When we finally got into the car, it was two minutes past ten. Since the service starts at ten and it takes fifteen minutes to drive there, we were late as usual. Mom wasn't going because she didn't feel good.

When we finally were seated in church, Vicki kept on turning around, pretending she was looking for someone, just so she could show herself to a guy who was sitting in the row behind. He was kind of goodlooking, but he was really old. He must have been at least twenty-five.

Finally Grandma pinched Vicki so she had to sit straight. After that she kept her face turned toward the window so the guy would be sure to see her profile. Vicki thinks she has a classic profile. When she told me, I said, "Yeah, sure. It goes all the way back to when we were apes." That shut her up for a while.

That night, after I had gone to bed, Dad came into my room. I was reading *Hawaii* by James Michener. I like his books because they are long and last me for a while. This was my third night with *Hawaii*, and I was only halfway through.

Dad sat down in my rocking chair very carefully. Arthur was stretched out on the floor, and he had one paw right under the chair. After Dad had moved the rocker out of the way, Arthur got up and walked over to the door. He knew he was being a bother, so he wanted out. Arthur still doesn't understand why Dad keeps on hanging around the house. The new kids don't bother him at all. It's just Dad. Dad says that if he ever wants a divorce, it will probably be because of Arthur.

After he had let the dog out, Dad said, "How is your project going?"

I put my book down. "Fine," I said. "But keeping track of what everybody is doing takes a lot of time."

Dad nodded understandingly. "All research projects are time-consuming. Just remember," he cautioned, "that in the end it might not work out the way you expect."

"Don't worry," I said, and yawned. "If everybody will just follow my advice, everything will be fine."

"Well," he said dryly, "you never know what to expect when you deal with human beings."

I smiled affectionately at him. "It's not the human beings I'm worried about," I said. "It's Vicki. Even Reverend Hayes was looking at her in church today. The way she acts is disgusting."

"She'll snap out of it eventually," Dad said soothingly. "It's just a phase she's going through."

"Hah," I said. "That's easy for you to say. You don't have to be around her all the time."

"Maybe you can have some influence on her after you move into her room."

"Sure," I said. And if you believe that, I thought, you must believe in the tooth fairy, too.

Sometimes parents can be terribly naïve.

Chapter 4

By Wednesday I was already halfway through my notebook, and after reading it, Mr. Campbell said, "I didn't know you had such a large family."

"It's going to be even larger," I said. "Mom is going to have a baby in a couple of weeks."

"I see." He paused. "Is everybody cooperating with your project?"

"I guess," I said reluctantly. "All I have done so far, anyway, is write down how much time they are using to do whatever they are doing. I might have problems later on."

He thought for a moment. Then he said. "Maybe you need to get them motivated. You know—make them want to change things for the better." He walked on to help Otis, who sits in front of me. "Think about it," he said over his shoulder.

I said I would.

Both Jenny and I had brought cold lunches so we could

sit outside. The weather has been just perfect this past week.

"How are you going to motivate them?" Jenny asked after we had settled down in the shade.

"I'll think of something," I said.

"My dad has a sign on his desk at the office that says 'Think Positive,'" Jenny said helpfully. "Maybe you could hang a sign on the front door that says 'Think Organized.'"

Right then Dennis Moreno walked past us. He grabbed Jenny's ponytail and pulled it until she fell backward and spilled most of her drink. Dennis is an eighth grader and a real bully.

Jenny sat up and said furiously, "Boy, I could kill that guy."

"Killing is too good for him," I said. "What he needs is a dose of his own medicine." I thought about it for a minute. "There must be something we can do . . . ."

"Like what?" Jenny finished her soda and squashed the can with her foot.

I smiled. Suddenly I had this super idea. "Like this." I told her what I had in mind, and we both went inside to get some stuff we needed.

When we were done, we had to walk around the whole building before we finally spotted Dennis. He was talking to a couple of fifth graders, and from what I could see he wasn't exactly being friendly either. Last year he was suspended for two weeks after he had forced about a dozen little kids to give him their lunch money. He had told them that if they didn't, he would beat them up.

Jenny and I pretended that we were so busy talking that we didn't see where we were going, and we practically walked into Dennis.

"Oh, *excuse* me," I said sweetly. Jenny giggled, and we

hurried off before he had a chance to say anything. Then we made a circle so we could see Dennis from behind. On the back of his shirt was a sign that said "My mother makes me wear diapers." We had used a black marking pen so the writing would stand out, and we had put lots of masking tape on the back of the paper to make sure it would stick to his clothes.

We both went into fits of laughter, and a minute later, when the bell rang, we followed Dennis inside. By now several other kids had seen it, too, and everybody was snickering.

"I hope nobody tells him about it," I said.

"Are you kidding? Nobody likes Dennis." Jenny was dragging me down the corridor so she could see what was happening.

Amanda Lewis, who is in Dennis's class, walked up to him and said with a deadpan face, "That's too bad. Especially at your age."

"My age what?" Dennis asked.

But Amanda swept past him into the classroom, her shoulders shaking. One of the other boys put his hand on Dennis's shoulder and said, "If you need any help changing, don't call on me." Then everybody started laughing, and somebody shut the door so we couldn't see what happened after that.

I was in my regular class for the rest of the afternoon, and every time Jenny turned around and looked at me we started giggling. I wondered how long it would be before Dennis found out.

When the last period was over, we didn't see him anywhere, and we had to go out so we wouldn't miss the bus. When I got off at the bottom of our driveway, I asked Jenny if she could come over after dinner. She thought she probably could.

"I thought we could make some posters to put up around the house," I said. "You know, like that sign you said your dad has on his desk?"

When we came inside, Ryan went straight into the family room and turned on the TV. He always watches first *Sesame Street* and then *Wonder Woman*. Meghan went to look for Grandma, and Vicki disappeared into the bathroom and locked the door. I set my stopwatch, wondering how long she'd stay there this time.

Jenny didn't come until seven because she had chores to do. The Reddingers are farmers, and Jenny and her brothers all have to do a lot of work around the place. Today it had been her turn to change the bedding for the horses.

I had already folded the laundry and done the dishes. Mom, who didn't feel like eating dinner, was painting. She has a corner of the family room set up as a studio. Mostly she works with watercolors. This is something she started doing after she got pregnant and had to give up some of her other activities. She is really very good, too.

"Maybe I should take up jogging again," she commented when I came to borrow some paper. "Then I could have the baby this week and I'd stop feeling sick all the time."

I shuddered. "Please don't," I said. "As soon as I have to move in with Vicki, *I'll* get sick." I picked up her large sketch pad. "Can I have some of this?"

"For what?"

I explained to her about the signs I wanted to make. She rummaged around in a box she had on the floor. "Here," she said. "You can use the back of these old drawings. I wasn't going to keep them anyway."

I had just gotten started when Jenny came. Vicki was

on the phone in the kitchen, and I had to leave my bedroom door open so I could hear when she was finished. She had already talked about absolutely nothing for more than half an hour.

Jenny and I worked hard for a while. Grandma brought us each a milk shake and said she was driving into town.

"Where are you going?" I asked.

"I have to buy some lottery tickets."

"I'll get you some tomorrow after school," I said. "I have an orthodontist appointment, and then I'm going to stay and wait for Dad."

"Tomorrow is too late." Grandma walked to the door. "But thanks anyway."

"What does she mean?" Jenny asked after Grandma had left. "The drawing isn't until next week."

I shrugged. "It probably says in her horoscope that she has to buy the tickets today," I said. "Or else she has had another premonition."

"Oh, that's right. I always forget."

Sometimes I read my horoscope, too. I'm a Taurus. The trouble is that different magazines have different predictions, so I don't see how you can believe in any of them. Even Grandma has problems with that sometimes. Once it said in the morning paper that this was the day she would find the thing she most desired at a bargain price. The horoscope in the weekly magazine, however, said that she'd better stay home and not make any unnecessary trips if she wanted to avoid accidents.

As a result, Grandma spent the whole day debating whether or not she should go shopping. When I asked her what it was that she most desired, she said she wasn't sure. Either it was the fabric she had been looking for to make herself a blouse, or it was a heating pad that she had been needing for the rheumatism in her leg, except she thought they were too expensive.

In the end she did go shopping after all, but she told me she was going to drive extra slowly, just in case. When she finally came home, all she had with her was a really sad-looking geranium. Grandma said she had forgotten that she had wanted one for her south window. When she walked into the store, there it was, priced down from four ninety-nine to ninety-nine cents, just because it was almost dead. After that she paid more attention to the horoscope in the newspaper.

After Jenny had gone home, I went around the house putting up my signs.

Over the kitchen sink it said "Happiness is getting the dishes done in twenty minutes." It never takes me more than twenty minutes, so there is no reason why it should take anybody else any longer.

On the bathroom door I put "Others have needs, too. Limit your visits to ten minutes." After looking at that for a moment, I changed my mind and took it down. After all, once you were inside the bathroom, you couldn't see it. Instead, I taped it up over the bathroom sink.

I had made two signs that read "Someone might be trying to reach you. Make your calls as short as possible." I put those up by the phones in the kitchen and family room. On the door to Vicki's room it said "Happiness is having a clean room," I didn't expect that one to stay up after Vicki had discovered it, but a least she would have read it once.

I had made half a dozen signs that read "Put everything in its proper place. Then you won't have to look for it." Those I put up all over the house.

Ryan and Marcus were playing with their electronic games in the living room. They were so wrapped up in their game that they didn't even notice I was watching. Ryan had a Popsicle in his mouth, and the red juice was dribbling down his chin.

"Where did you get that?" I asked.

Ryan looked up. He took the Popsicle out of his mouth. "Get what?"

"The Popsicle?"

"I borrowed Jerry's Popsicle maker. He said I can keep it for a week." Jerry is Jenny's brother.

"Can I have one?"

"Have what?"

I sighed. Sometimes Ryan drives me crazy. "A Popsicle, of course."

Ryan shook his head.

"How come? It makes eight at a time."

"I only have four left."

"Who ate the other four?"

"I did. I'll have the rest for breakfast tomorrow." He took a big lick. "I made then from stawberry pop. They are yummy." He patted his stomach.

I went to my room and made a sign that said "Happiness is sharing." I taped it on the mirror in the boys' room. Then I went to bed. Vicki wasn't home yet. She was out on a date with Harry.

Arthur, who was stretched out on the floor, started snoring. I turned off the light and tried to go to sleep. After ten minutes I got up again and woke Arthur up. I gave him an old bone to chew on.

It was quiet for about five minutes, and then the snoring started again. I pulled the blankets over my head. Maybe I'll buy some earplugs.

Chapter 5

At breakfast I asked innocently, "What did you do with the sign I put on your door, Vicki?"

"Nobody sticks anything on my door without asking me first," she said coldly.

"How could I ask? You weren't home."

Vicki gave me a murderous look.

Dad cleared his throat. "I think we all should do our best to support Karen's project," he said. He glanced at Vicki. "It might do us all some good to try to use our time a little more . . . er . . . productively."

"I told her not to bug me," Vicki murmured, her mouth full of food.

"The least you can do is leave her signs alone," Dad said diplomatically. "What did it say anyway?"

Marcus snickered. "'Happiness is a clean room,'" he said. "I guess Vicki doesn't know what that means."

"It's *my* room," she snapped.

I poured some more syrup on my French toast. "Soon it will be *our* room," I said dreamily. "I can't wait. I always wanted to live in a garbage dump."

Vicki jumped up from her chair. "Did you hear that?" she cried. "And you expect me to live with her? Don't I have any rights anymore?"

She pushed the long blond hair out of her face and threw the napkin on the floor.

When she started to leave, Dad said sternly, "Sit down, Vicki." Vicki stopped and turned around. "Sit down," Dad repeated. I could tell by the tone of his voice that he really meant business, and I guess Vicki could, too, because she sank down on the chair again. Dad is pretty easygoing most of the time, but once in a while, when he gets really angry, he puts his foot down. He was angry now.

Grandma got up and started to clear the table. Mom was still in bed. She feels sick most mornings and doesn't want to eat. Other women get sick during the first months of their pregnancy, but Mom was perfectly fine until the last few weeks. That's when she started to feel queasy and had trouble keeping food down.

"I'm glad Mom isn't down here," Dad said in a tight voice. "She doesn't need another thing to upset her." He fastened his eyes on Vicki. "I should have done something about this earlier, but I thought you'd shape up by yourself. Obviously you haven't. I know you have had extra chores lately, but so has everybody else. The others haven't complained while you have been whining and griping about everything. Grandma has done more than her share of household chores because she'd rather do things herself than put up with your lousy attitude and bad temper.

"Karen has been very good about having to give up her room," he continued. "If anyone has a reason to complain, it's she. I'm afraid her description of your room is very fitting, and I'll give you until Sunday night to do something about it. And," he added, "until your room is straightened up, you're not allowed to go anywhere or have any of your friends over. Karen will move her things in Monday. I want this settled before your mother has to go in to the hospital. I don't want her to worry about it while she is gone."

There was a moment's silence while everybody looked at Vicki. Marcus opened his mouth to say something, but after a warning glance from Dad he shut it again.

"Well?" Dad said ominously. "Is that understood?"

"All right, all right," Vicki said sourly. "Can I go now?"

Dad nodded, and Vicki stalked out of the kitchen.

"She has a date with Elroy Saturday night," I said informatively.

Dad grunted. "Maybe they are planning to elope," he said hopefully.

"What's 'elope'?" Ryan asked.

"That's when you run away to get married," I explained.

"Elroy told me he has to be home by midnight or he'll get grounded," Ryan said seriously. He looked puzzled when everybody started laughing.

School was out at one o'clock because all the teachers were attending a seminar. Instead of going home with the bus, Jenny and I went to the library. Jenny's mother was supposed to pick us up at two o'clock.

Sometimes we take our bikes to school instead of

riding the bus; but mine had a flat tire, and Dad hadn't gotten around to fixing it yet. We live only a mile from town anyway, and if it hadn't been for all the books we had to carry, we would have walked home.

We were just done checking out our books when Mrs. Gordon told Jenny that her mother was on the phone. Mrs. Gordon is the librarian.

"I bet she can't pick us up," Jenny said darkly.

"Don't be so negative. She might just be late." Jenny always assumes the worst.

When she came back, she said triumphantly, "I told you she wouldn't be able to pick us up. The car wouldn't start. I guess we'll have to walk. She said Dad will stop on his way home and pick up our books."

Mrs. Gordon put all our books in a tote bag and placed it under the counter. "I'll make sure he gets it," she promised.

We were about halfway home when Jenny pointed up the hill. "Look, somebody is moving into the Patterson house."

The Pattersons built this gorgeous house a few years ago, about half a mile from where we live. The whole front is glass, and it looks like something from *Better Homes and Gardens*.

Then last spring they moved to Alaska, and the house was put up for sale. Dad said it would never sell because of the price, and it had been vacant all summer.

Now there was a moving van parked in the yard, and some men were carrying furniture inside.

We stopped and watched for a few minutes.

"I wonder if they have any kids," I said.

"Probably. I mean, the house is so big. There are at least four bedrooms, and the family room is huge." Jenny knows the house a lot better than I because her oldest sister used to baby-sit for the Pattersons. "People don't buy something that size unless they have children."

"Maybe Grandma can made a cake and bring it over," I said as we started walking again. "And I could go with her."

"If they do have kids, they'll be riding the bus," Jenny pointed out.

"Yeah," I said. "I guess we'll find out on Monday."

As soon as I came home, I practiced the piano for an hour. The boys were outside, playing ball, and Vicki was in her room, making lots of noise. I guess she had started digging into her mess. Mom and Grandma had gone to the supermarket, and Meghan was playing house with the cats.

We have six cats. Four of them were ours before we came to this house, and two are Grandma's. Meghan loves them, and Moms says she must be communicating with them in some special way because they do everything she tells them to do. I have watched her putting them down on the floor in a circle, one at a time and telling them to stay, and they stay.

Meghan has a room of her own which really used to be a walk-in closet. It's only big enough for her bed and a chair and a dresser. Most of the cats sleep with her at night, and after the light has been turned off, she keeps on talking to them until she falls asleep.

Today is my last day for timing everybody. Now I have to come up with some ideas to help them get organized.

I walked around the house to make sure all the signs were still there, and then I picked up the toys that were scattered around in the hall.

When I opened the door to the hall closet, which is where everybody puts everything, it was so jammed with stuff that there wasn't room for one more thing.

Obviously it needed some reorganizing, too. And if *I* didn't do it, I guessed nobody else would.

Just the thought of all that work made me hungry. I went to the kitchen and made two peanut butter sandwiches. Then I started emptying out the closet. It was unbelievable how much junk there was.

It reminded me of a magic show I had been to once where the magician pulled yards and yards of fabric out of a cylinder that was about the size of a pencil. You could have sworn there was no way all that fabric could ever have fitted into it.

When I had taken everything out of the closet, I felt the same. There were enough things on the hall floor to fill a garage. Among all the stuff I found the tennis ball I had been looking for since summer and my other red mitten that I was sure had been lost on the school bus.

Mom and Grandma came home just when I was in the middle of sorting everything into piles. There was a pile for each member of the family, one pile with things to be thrown away, and one pile with stuff that belonged in the garage.

"Oh, look!" Mom exclaimed. "There is my silk scarf. I've been wondering what happened to it." She put it around her neck, looking very pleased.

Grandma picked up her muff and turned it around, frowning. "I wonder why this wasn't put in mothballs."

"Probably because it has been years since anyone cleaned out this closet," I said.

At dinnertime Mom asked Vicki if she had gotten her math test back yet. Vicki said she had. She got only a D−.

"It sounds as if you need to spend more time on your studies," Dad said.

Vicki sighed theatrically and said she would have done better if she hadn't had to baby-sit at the Greys' the night before the test.

While she was talking, I opened my notebook, which I had on my lap. "You could have studied before you went to the Greys'," I said.

Vicki gave me a dark look. "It was my turn to do the dishes, remember?"

I put the fork down and consulted my notes again. "I know," I said, "but you finished them at ten minutes to seven, and then you watched TV until eight. And before dinner you spent forty minutes talking to Debbie on the phone, and before that—"

Dad cleared his throat. "That's enough, Karen," he said.

Vicki looked like she was ready to kill me. I gave her one of my innocent stares and stuffed the rest of my sandwich in my mouth. Vicki was just going to say something when Dad spoke.

"I think Karen has a point there, Vicki. You are just not utilizing your time. Considering how close you were to a failing grade last semester, you really should make an effort to catch up. And," he added wearily, "I understand math isn't the only subject you have trouble with either."

Starting next week, Vicki has to do homework between three-thirty and five-thirty every day. That means she can't make phone calls or watch TV or do anything else during that time.

Before I went to bed, I stuck one of my 'Put everything where it belongs' signs on the door of the hall closet. Tomorrow I am going to straighten up the bookcase in the family room. Mrs. Gordon told me Marcus has thirteen overdue books, and I bet a lot of them are in there. He is blacklisted until he has returned all the books.

I was just going to turn off the light by my bed when someone knocked on my door.

"Karen, are you sleeping?"

Without waiting for an answer, Grandma came in. She was carrying a magazine.

"What are you planning to do tomorrow?" she asked.

I sat up in bed and stifled a yawn. "I'm not sure. Did you know that someone has moved into the Patterson house?"

"Oh, really?" For a moment she looked interested, but then she remembered why she had come. She held up the magazine, which was opened to the page that had the horoscope. She started reading. "It says here, "The health of a family member is threatened this weekend. Be extra careful."

I yawned again. "Don't worry," I said. "It must be Vicki they are talking about. She'll probably drop into a dead faint when she finally is able to see her floor again." I hugged my knees. "Are you going to bring something over?"

"Over where?" Grandma asked.

"To our new neighbors, of course," I said patiently. "If you do, can I go with you?"

Grandma opened the door. "I'll think about it," she said. "Go to sleep now. Good night."

When I reached for the light, I discovered that Arthur was missing. In fact, I didn't remember having seen him since before dinner.

I got out of bed and walked barefoot through the kitchen and out the back door. It was dark outside and quiet. The moon was up, and I could see the outline of the trees. Over by the tool shed was a dark shadow. I tiptoed through the grass, which was already wet from the dew.

Arthur was sitting very quietly, staring out over the pasture. He didn't even move when I put my arms around him. Sometimes I think he is more human than some people I know.

"It's time to go inside." I said softly.

Arthur turned his head and put his wet nose against my cheek. Then he sighed, a long, deep sigh. Obediently he walked behind me back to the house. His big paws made a swooshing sound in the wet grass.

Chapter 6

It took Vicki until Sunday afternoon to clean up her room. Dad went in and checked, and then he helped move my furniture. Vicki's room is pretty big, but after my bed and dresser were in place, the only spot left for my bookcase was alongside the bed.

"Why don't you just leave it downstairs?" Dad suggested. "Obviously there isn't enough room for it here."

"But I need my books all the time," I protested. "Besides, if it's down there everybody gets into it, and all my books will get ruined."

The only problem with having the bookcase alongside my bed was that I couldn't get to what was on the bottom shelf without moving the whole bookcase. I solved that by putting all the stuff I hardly ever read on that shelf.

When I was done, I thought it looked kind of neat. The bookcase is almost as wide as my bed is long, and it blocks my view of Vicki's side of the room. It's almost like having a dividing wall.

The bookcase isn't very tall, but I lined up all my potted plants on the top; that helped. I have seven plants right now, but I also have some cuttings in water which should be rooting soon. My favorite is a large white geranium which is in bloom.

In my old room I had most of them by the window since they need lots of light, but here there isn't any window space. If they don't do all right on the bookcase, I'll have to move them back downstairs. I'd hate to see them die.

As soon as Dad told Vicki that her room looked all right, she rode her bike to town to see Debbie. Debbie is okay, but I can't understand why she puts up with my sister. I sure wouldn't if I were her.

It was just as well that Vicki wasn't home while I moved my things because I wasn't in the mood to listen to any of her cute remarks. While she was gone, I opened her closet to see what it looked like. There were so many clothes jammed on the rack that I couldn't even squeeze my hand in between. On the floor were three large boxes piled with shoes. I guess that's Vicki's idea of a neat closet.

When I asked Mom to come look, she said that considering whose closet it was, it was a miracle of orderliness. She pointed out that even the door could be shut now.

"I bet she never wears half of her stuff," I said.

"Well," Mom said diplomatically, "at least she can't say she has nothing to wear."

I put Arthur's blanket down on the floor between my bed and the wall. There is just enough room for him to stretch out. I hope he won't get too upset tonight when he finds out we have moved.

When I was done with the room, I went outside for a while. The weather has been really nice the last few days, but it's finally beginning to look like fall. The trees are turning red and yellow, and despite the sunshine, the air is kind of chilly.

Fall is my favorite season. I like winter, too, when there is enough snow so I can go skiing. Some winters there isn't. When I grow up, I might homestead up in Alaska. That's about the only place where you can still get a piece of land for nothing, as long as you build a house on it and live there.

Marcus and Jonathan were playing softball down by the creek. Jonathan is Jenny's brother. Ryan was roller-skating on the concrete in front of the garage. I went inside to see if Dad had fixed my bike yet, but of course, he hadn't. I'd patch the inner tube myself if I could get the tire off, but I can't. I've tried.

"Weren't you supposed to take the garbage out?" I asked Ryan. It's his chore to empty the kitchen trash into the can in the tool shed, and I knew for a fact that there were two grocery bags overflowing with garbage in the kitchen.

Ryan was trying to skate backward without falling. "I'll do it tomorrow," he said without looking up. "I'm busy right now."

"You'd better do it before Grandma gets up from her nap," I warned. "You know she's going to get mad."

"I don't see why I always have to take the garbage out," he complained. He leaned too far backward and fell. He licked his hand, which had got scratched on the concrete. "Why don't you leave me alone? I can't practice when somebody is watching."

"I'll trade you," I said. "I'll do the garbage and you can do the vacuuming instead."

Ryan glared at me. "What for? Vacuuming is your job. I'd rather not do any chores at all."

"Sure," I said sarcastically. "You hardly ever do any, anyway. Maybe I'll start with you tomorrow."

"Start what?"

"Getting you organized, dummy. Tomorrow is when I'll tell everybody what to do. You can be first."

"Big deal," he muttered. When I left, he hit the garage wall and fell again. He was wearing my roller skates from last year, and they are too big for him, even though he wears three pairs of socks.

When I came in, I opened my TES journal and wrote down some observations about my project. Then I started a new page. I put Ryan's name at the top, and then I listed the areas where he needed to improve. There weren't that many. Ryan isn't quite as bad as Marcus, and of course, nobody is anywhere as bad as Vicki. I'm not looking forward to talking to her. But at least she can't lock herself in her room anymore.

Chapter 7

There were no new kids on the bus. Jenny and I looked up at the Patterson house as we drove by. A car and a truck were parked in the yard.

"Is your grandmother going to go there?" Jenny asked.

"I don't know. What about your mother?"

"I forgot to tell her about it." She changed the subject. "Are you moving into Vicki's room today?"

I told her I already had. Then I said, "Vicki complained to Dad this morning that she didn't get any sleep because of Arthur, and why couldn't he sleep outside like other dogs?"

"What did your dad say?" Jenny asked interestedly.

"He told her to stick some cotton in her ears," I said smugly. "He said that if I could put up with Arthur, there was no reason why she couldn't." I giggled. "Then he reminded her what happened last time we tried to get Arthur to sleep outside."

"You mean, the time he broke the kitchen door?"

"Yeah."

I had also told Vicki that the dogs behaved better in the house than she did, but then Dad said that was enough and he didn't want to hear any more bickering.

We had a social studies test that was really easy, and after that we had to go to band rehearsal. I play the clarinet, and I'm getting pretty good at it. The sixth, seventh, and eighth graders play together, and so far we sound pretty awful. We are practicing for the Chirstmas concert, which will take place the first week of December. I hope we'll sound better by then.

When practice was over, Mr. Donovan, who is our music teacher, asked if I would like to play a piano solo at the concert. I said I probably would, so he gave me a choice of four different things to play. I have until next month to decide which one I like best.

The pavement in the school parking lot was all torn up because some water pipes are being replaced, and all the buses had to park by the football field. That meant I had to run across the field since our bus is at the very end.

Because I forgot my sneakers, I had to go back to the gym, and then I was late, of course. Running across the field, I slipped and fell and got grass stains all over my new San Francisco jeans. The bus had just started to move when I stumbled on board, and I just barely avoided falling in Tommy Olsen's lap. When I finally sank down beside Jenny, I was so out of breath I thought I'd have a heart attack.

Jenny looked critically at my jeans. "I bet that won't come off in the wash," she said.

"It'd better," I gasped. "These are my best pants."

Vicki, who was sitting across the aisle, said cattily, "I told Mom she shouldn't have bought them. I knew something like this would happen."

I stared disgustedly at her. She is jealous because I got a pair when they were on sale and she didn't. They had only small sizes left.

Mom had made cupcakes for a snack, and I grabbled one on my way through the kitchen.

Ryan dropped his books on the floor. "You took the one I wanted," he complained.

I looked at the cupcakes. "They are all the same."

"They are not either. You took the only green one, and you know green is my favorite color."

I shrugged. "So what? That doesn't mean that you should have it all the time. Besides, the icing is the same." I took a bite. "She only uses different food coloring."

Ryan scraped off some of the pink icing on his. He licked his finger. "It's not the same," he protested. "I don't like this kind." He took another lick, and then he stuffed the whole cupcake in his mouth.

I looked at him. "If you don't like it, why are you eating it?" I asked. He looked really disgusting with his cheeks all bulging.

"I'm hungry," he mumbled indistinctly. "I didn't get seconds for lunch."

I sighed and went to my room. Vicki had thrown her books on the floor by my bed. I kicked them over to her side of the room. It was hard to believe she had cleaned only yesterday. Already there was stuff all over the place.

First I changed into another pair of pants so I could put my jeans in to soak. I didn't want to take any chances. I hoped the stains would come out. Then I took my notebook and a pencil and went to the boys' room. Marcus was on the top bunk, playing with an electronic game, and Ryan was running his remote-control car on the floor. They didn't even look up when I came in.

I noticed that the mirror was empty.

"Where is the sign I put up?" I asked.

"What sign?" Marcus kicked off his sneakers. One of them fell on the car.

"Watch it, will you?" Ryan yelled.

"What happened to the sign?" I asked again.

"What sign?" This time it was Ryan. He gave me an innocent look.

"You know what sign," I said patiently. "Didn't you hear what Dad said about leaving them alone?"

"I didn't take it down," Marcus said.

"Not me either."

I decided to drop the subject. Instead, I sat down on the chair and opened my notebook. "Now, I want you to listen," I said. "Put away your toys and pay attention."

"I'm listening," Marcus said. He didn't even look up from his game.

"I wasn't talking to you," I said coldly. "I'm doing Ryan first." I stood up again. "Come on," I said to Ryan. "Let's go somewhere else."

When I came out in the hall, I stuck my head back through the door. "Why don't you go wash your feet?" I said to Marcus. "They stink."

Ryan and I went into the den. Normally we're not allowed in there because Dad has papers and things that he doesn't want anybody to touch, but he said I could use it while I was working on my project.

Ryan put his car down on the floor. I picked it up and hid it behind my back.

"Hey," he cried, "that's my car. Give it back."

"After we are done," I said. I put the car under the desk. "First let's talk about your chores."

"I don't have any chores today," he said quickly.

"You do, too. What about making your bed in the morning?"

He squirmed. "I don't have time."

I sighed. "Of course you do. It shouldn't take you more than fifteen minutes to make your bed, get dressed, and pick up your room. That leaves half an hour for eating breakfast."

Ryan was playing with his shoelaces. "I have to stand in line to go to the bathroom, and that takes lots of time," he said complainingly. "Especially when I wake up. And I hardly ever have time to brush my teeth."

I grunted and chewed on my pen. He had a point there. One bathroom just isn't enough for that many people. There is Grandma's, of course, but we all can't run across the yard to her place all the time.

"Okay," I said. "What if you start getting up a little earlier instead?" I thought about it for a moment. "That way you boys would be up before Vicki and me, and you could use the bathroom first. How's that?"

His face brightened. "I guess that's okay."

"Good." I looked at my notes. "Now, about the garbage. Why don't you take it out first thing when you get home from school? That way you won't forget about it later." I gave him an encouraging look.

Now Ryan was busy peeling a scab off his arm. "Did you know it has taken over two weeks for this to heal?" He held the scab up to show me.

"Never mind," I said irritably. "Did you hear what I said?"

"About what?"

I took a deep breath and counted to five. "About the

garbage. Take it out as soon as you come home from school."

"What about my snack?"

"You can eat that after you take the trash out."

"But I'm always starving when I come home."

I gritted my teeth. "All right, all right. Eat your snack first, and then take out the trash."

"What if I forget?"

"Well, don't," I said sharply. Then I added, "I'll remind you until you get used to it, okay?"

He was still fiddling with his arm.

"Is that okay?" I repeated.

"I guess so." He looked up. "Can I go now?"

"Not yet," I said. "If you have to play your dumb electronic games, can you do it while Dad is still at work? You know how he hates that sound."

"What if I want to play before I go to bed?"

I rolled my eyes. "Then do it in your room instead of in the living room. At least he can't hear it then." I consulted my notes again. "And put your dirty clothes in the laundry instead of stuffing them under your bed."

Ryan looked uncomfortable. "You sound like Grandma," he said.

I ignored that. "I'll write these things on a paper for you and put it over your bed," I said. "That way you can check yourself. How's that?"

"What do I get if I'm good?"

I sighed again. "If you do all right this week, I'll treat you to an ice cream on Saturday," I said.

Then I gave him back his car and asked him to tell Marcus to come in. While I was waiting, I went to the bathroom. For once nobody was there. When I came back to the den, Marcus was playing with Dad's calculator.

"You'd better put that back," I said. "Dad will kill you if you break it."

Marcus gave me a superior look. "He'll kill *you* when he finds out you're using the den."

"I have permission," I said coldly.

For a moment I thought about where to start.

"Hurry up," Marcus said impatiently. "I have things to do." He added, "Why did you pick such a dumb project anyway?"

Talking to Marcus was mostly a repeat of what I'd said to Ryan. Marcus is supposed to do the dinner dishes once a week, but half the time he isn't even around to do it. The same thing happens when it's his turn to clean the bathroom.

"Don't you realize that every time you skip your chores somebody else gets stuck with them?" I said. "Last time you skipped the bathroom, Grandma cleaned it for you."

"So what?" Marcus yawned. "She does a better job than I do."

"How can you say something like that?" I cried hotly. "She has enough work to do without doing your chores, too."

Marcus looked a little embarrased. "Okay," he muttered. "I promise I'll clean when it's my turn."

I felt guilty myself when I thought of how I had suggested Grandma should find something constructive to do. That was only a week ago, but since then I had discovered that she is the one who does most of the work at our house. Normally Mom cooks our meals, but these last few weeks she hasn't been able even to smell food without feeling sick, so Grandma has had to do the cooking, too.

At least Marcus agreed that it would help if he and

Ryan got up fifteen minutes earlier in the morning. He also promised to put his dirty clothes in the laundry every day instead of dumping a whole mountain on the utility room floor every Friday. That's what everybody seems to do, and that's why the washing machine runs nonstop all Saturday.

After I was done with Marcus, I stretched out on the floor in the family room to go over my notes. I was pretty happy with what I had done so far. I was saving Vicki for tomorrow.

Ryan was watching *Wonder Woman*, and Mom was keeping him company while she was doing some mending. Meghan was on the couch, rocking one of the cats to sleep.

I looked with satisfaction at the bookcase, which is neater than it has ever been before. It's actually built-in shelving that covers the whole south wall of the family room. If there's one thing we have too much of in this house, it's books, believe me. We have boxes and boxes of books in the basement, too. Those are Mom's, which she had before she got married. There was simply no room for them anywhere, so I guess they'll stay packed until we move again.

When I cleaned out the shelves last week, I found a lot of interesting things like seven overdue library books. One was due two years ago. That turned out to be Vicki's. She had to pay for the book a long time ago when she couldn't find it. Now she is taking it back to see if she'll get her money refunded.

I also found the music sheet with the bridal march that Grandma said she'd been looking for for ages and two photos that Ryan said were of their cousins, which must have been there for years.

Mom helped me sort the books. One *Reader's Digest*

Condensed Books volume had a banana peel stuck between the pages which was so dried in that Mom had to tear the pages out to get rid of it. Of course, nobody admitted to having left the peel there.

When I asked Mom why she even bothered to try to find out who the guilty person was, she laughed and said it was habit. If anyone should suddenly own up to something, she'd probably drop dead from the shock.

At six-thirty Marcus and Ryan and Meghan and I were picked up by Jenny and her dad. We were going to Freewater to see *E.T.* Timberline doesn't even have a movie theater.

The last time *E.T.* was showing I saw it three times in a row. I still think it's the best movie I have ever seen, so I didn't want to miss out this time either. It's supposed to run for only a week.

Ryan didn't want to go because he thought it was some kind of monster movie, but I practically forced him to come along because I knew he'd love it.

Meghan couldn't wait to go because she has had my big *E.T.* doll for a long time, and she thinks it's another animal.

Remembering how much I cried last time, I brought lots of Kleenex. Jenny couldn't find any before she left home, so she brought a washcloth instead. I ran out of tissues before the end of the movie when Elliot says good-bye to E.T., which is the saddest part, and I ended up using one end of her washcloth. Ryan cried so hard he got the hiccups, and Meghan couldn't understand why she couldn't bring E.T. home to live with us.

Jenny and I might go see it again later this week if her brother will drive us.

Chapter 8

We had just started our first period, which was English, when Miss Stevens was called to the office. Miss Stevens is our teacher in English and history.

As soon as she left, everybody started talking and playing. Eric took a baseball out of his backpack and threw it across the room to Larry. Larry tossed it back, and when Eric tried to catch it, he fell over somebody's desk and knocked it down. The ball hit the wall and knocked down an African drum that was hanging there.

Lee was just putting the drum back when the door opened. Miss Stevens stood still for a moment, surveying the classroom. She had probably heard the noise. Eric was finishing getting the desk back up. His face was red. Miss Stevens looked at him in silence. Then she spotted the ball, which was on the floor, and she went over and got it. Still without saying anything, she walked up to her desk and put the ball in her purse. I'm sure she had figured out that the ball was Eric's, and anyway, we all knew he wouldn't get it back.

She had told us the first day of school that anyone who was caught playing with a toy or whatever during class time would lose it. She would put a price on it, and whoever owned it would have the opportunity to buy it back a week later. The money would be used for the next upcoming class party. If the confiscated item was not bought back, it would be returned at the end of the semester.

Two years ago, when Marcus was in her class, Miss Stevens confiscated this particular magazine she found on the floor in the classroom. When she said the price would be two dollars, nobody came forward to buy it back, and at the end of the semester no one claimed it either. Marcus told me he knew whose magazine it was, but he didn't want to tell. When I asked what happened to things that weren't claimed, he said Miss Stevens gave them to Goodwill, but he didn't think she'd give them this particular magazine.

When the class was quiet again, Miss Stevens announced that we were getting a new student. His name was Andy Miller, and he would be in as soon as he was through at the office. He had just moved here from Texas, and Miss Stevens wanted all of us to help him feel at home.

She had barely finished talking when the door opened again and this new kid came in. He was rather tall and had blond hair and a terrific tan. He looked kind of cute.

I glanced at Jenny, and she raised her eyebrows and mouthed something I couldn't understand. Miss Stevens told Andy he could have Jeremy's desk for today since Jeremy was absent and she'd get him another desk tomorrow.

Everybody stared at the newcomer, of course, and he stared back at us. He didn't seem shy or self-conscious at all. I'm not sure I would be able to act that casual if I had to move to a school where I didn't know anybody.

Jenny passed on a note to me that said, "Does he live in the Patterson house?" I put it in my pocket before Miss Stevens could see it.

Andy was sitting only two spaces away from me, and as soon as the bell rang, I went over and touched his shoulder.

"Hi," I said when he turned around. "I'm Karen Carlson."

"Hi." When he smiled, I noticed that he had really beautiful teeth.

"Did you just move to town?" I asked.

Miss Stevens had just told us that, of course, but I couldn't think of anything else to say right then.

"Yeah. Last week."

"Where do you live?"

"About half a mile outside town. We bought a house." He had dreamy blue eyes, too, with really dark eyelashes.

"Did you buy it from a family named Patterson?" I asked. "And is the front of the house all glass?"

He looked surprised. "Yes. How did you know?"

I smiled mysteriously. "A little bird told me." I was suddenly glad I was wearing my new jeans and my matching blue and white sweater.

Andy gave me another smile. "No, honestly," he said. "How did you know?"

Jenny was hanging onto my arm. Her face was all red.

She goes absolutely dumb when she meets new people. Especially boys.

"We noticed that somebody had moved in there," I explained. "That is, Jenny and I did." I pushed Jenny forward, and her face got even redder. "This is my best friend Jenny Reddinger. We live on the same road as you. Our house is about half a mile away, and Jenny lives next to us."

Jenny started giggling. She always does that when she is nervous. "That's right. We're all neighbors. How do you like your new house? Isn't it gorgeous? I mean, especially the living room. And the bedrooms, too, of course." She stopped her babbling and went into another fit of giggles. I was glad I wasn't her.

Jenny is usually all right, but on occasions like this she always acts like a two-year-old. It's pretty embarrassing.

"How come we didn't see you on the bus?" I said.

Andy shrugged. "I rode with my brother. He has his own car." Then he added, "I'll probably ride the bus some of the time, though."

"How old is your brother?"

"Seventeen. He is a senior."

"What's his name?"

"Roger."

I wondered if his brother was good-looking, too. Anyway, it would blow Vicki's mind to have a senior practically next door even if he looked like Dracula.

"Do you have any other brothers or sisters?"

"I have one brother who is at UCLA and two sisters who are married. They live out East."

Jenny giggled again. "I guess that means you are the baby in the family," she said.

I could have clobbbered her. Sometimes she doesn't have any manners at all. Fortunately Andy didn't get mad. He just nodded and said, "I guess it does." I thought he acted very mature.

Then Miss Stevens came and said we had to go outside. I had to run because I was supposed to have been downstairs in Mr.Campbell's class five minutes ago. When I left, Jenny was still standing there with a silly grin on her face.

I couldn't wait for three o'clock to come around so I could see if Andy was on the bus. Just for once I was early, and the bus just came in when I got to the parking lot. Jenny came right after me. She looked normal again; that was a relief. I can't stand her when she goes to pieces.

Andy didn't show. Maybe he'll be on the bus tomorrow.

After I was done practicing the piano, Mom and I played a game of checkers. She asked me how my project was going. I told her I really needed her help to get Saturday morning breakfast straightened out.

"What's the problem?" she asked.

I stared at the board and tried to remember which piece I had intended to move. "The problem is that everybody gets up at a different time and makes a different thing to eat," I explained. "You know. And then the kitchen is a mess, and it takes Grandma an hour to clean up so she can make lunch," I added. "Not that anybody should need lunch anyway."

"Hmmm," Mom said absentmindedly. "That's an idea. Not to have lunch, I mean. Since everybody has a late breakfast, they should get by with just a snack." She moved first one piece and then another one, and then she put both of them back again.

"You're not supposed to do that," I said.

I always tell her that, and she always does it anyway. It

really taxes my patience to play with Mom because she has such a hard time making up her mind where to go. As disorganized as she is, I often wonder how on earth she managed to graduate from vet school. When I asked her once what her grades were, I found out that she had been the top student in her class. That really blew my mind.

It wasn't that I didn't think she was smart enough to be in the top, but I could imagine her never finding her books so she could study and always losing her notes and things like that.

Like I said, you have to have patience when you play a game with her. Of course, she's not quite as bad as Grandma. *She* starts every move by circling her hand over the board, waiting for some inner voice to tell her what to do. She does it with her eyes closed so she won't be distracted. One game with her takes forever.

Mom and I didn't finish our game because Ryan came in with a scraped knee. He had bled through his jeans. After Mom had cleaned it and put a bandage on, she told him that was the end of roller-skating until the knee healed up.

"Did you notice that I took the garbage out?" Ryan asked after Mom had gone.

I said I did. I had checked his room in the morning, too. Last night I tacked a reminder list over his bed.

Ryan walked stiff-legged into the kitchen. "How many days do I have to do chores to get my ice cream?" he asked.

"The rest of the week, of course." I added warningly. "If you miss as much as one day, you won't get any."

Ryan's face lit up. "You mean, from now on I get ice cream every Saturday?"

"Of course not," I said indignantly. "Only this week

until you get used to doing your chores properly."

He looked hopefully at me. "It will take me lots of weeks to get used to it."

"Only this week," I repeated.

Ryan looked disappointed.

"There is no way I would buy you ice cream every week anyway," I said. "Besides, you should be doing your chores without anybody having to tell you or give you something. We all live here, so we all have to help, you know."

"Says who?"

Without even answering, I went upstairs. I wondered what kind of mood Vicki was in. I tiptoed over to the door so she wouldn't hear me. She was supposed to be doing her homework, but I was ready to bet she wasn't.

I was right. When I opened the door, she pushed her romance book under the bed and grabbed the dictionary. I pretended I hadn't seen anything.

For my life I can't understand how Vicki can read these romances all the time. I've read some of them, and believe me, they are the pits. Like they say, if you've read one, you've read them all.

I can't see any point in reading a book when you already know how it is going to end. When I pointed that out to Vicki, she said I was too young to understand. But if you ask me, she is the one who doesn't understand.

The romance books all have different authors, but I think they all are written by a computer and then the publisher makes up all these fictitious names to put on the covers.

At five-thirty Vicki shoved her school stuff over in a corner and started combing her hair. I stood up so I could look over the bookcase. "I need to talk to you about my project." I said.

She didn't even turn around. "I told you not to bug me," she said.

"Dad says that everybody is supposed to cooperate."

"You don't say," she said coldly.

"Okay," I said nonchalantly. "Have it your way." I walked over to the door. Grandma was banging on a pot downstairs. That's her way of announcing that dinner is ready.

Before I closed the door behind me, I said, "I bet Dad would like to find out that you've been reading your romance book instead of doing your homework."

Vicki swung around. She was furious, but she knew I had the upper hand, so she swallowed whatever she was going to say. "I'll give you ten minutes after dinner," she muttered.

I gave her a brilliant smile. "Well, thank you," I said sweetly. "I'll try not to take too much of your valuable time."

It's too bad you can't donate people to Goodwill.

Chapter 9

To get a positive answer out of Vicki about my project was like pulling teeth. Yes, she liked living in a dump, and what business was that of mine anyway? No, she didn't care about her grades. No, she didn't think she was using the bathroom more than anybody else. No, she hardly ever called anybody, and if somebody called her, she couldn't be expected to hang up, could she? Besides *we* weren't paying for the phone call.

There was a long silence. Vicki was busy chewing gum and filing her long red fingernails.

I chewed on my pencil and tried to think of what to say next. After all, Vicki was my main target. If it hadn't been for her, I wouldn't even have started this project. But obviously I wasn't getting anywhere with her.

For the first time I felt really discouraged. The whole

thing had seemed so straightforward and easy. I remembered what Dad had said about the result's not coming out the way I'd want it to. Maybe he was right.

I was still wondering what to do when Vicki suddenly jumped up from her chair. "Time's up," she said, and before I had time to open my mouth, she disappeared out the door.

A moment later the door opened again, and Dad stuck his head in. "Are you all done?" he asked.

I was really glad to see him. "Yeah, I'm all done," I said bitterly. "And so is my project. I should have picked something else." I let Dad have his chair back, and instead, I sat down cross-legged on the carpet.

Dad looked at me sympathetically. "I gather something has gone wrong," he said. "Care to tell me about it?"

After I was done explaining everything, Dad scratched his head and looked out the window. He didn't say anything, but I knew he was thinking about what I had said.

That's what I like most about him. He doesn't brush you off when you tell him about something, and he doesn't give you a pat answer either. He always thinks about it before answering, and usually what he has to say makes sense. He reminds me of Gordon. When Mom and I lived at our old house, I used to go to Gordon with my problems, and he really helped me lots of times. A lot of grown-ups act as if the problems we kids have aren't really important, but Gordon never did. Dad doesn't either. He still hadn't said anything, but just from having told him about it I felt better.

Finally Dad turned to me and said, "You still want to finish the project, don't you?"

I nodded reluctantly. "I guess so," I said. "Only what

do I do when nobody really wants to get organized?"

Dad leaned over his desk. "Let me get one thing straight first," he said. "This project is called a Time Efficiency Study, am I right?"

When I nodded, he continued. "That means that it's a study, which means that what you are supposed to do is to record data and make observations and note any changes that may occur, right?"

I nodded again, although I wasn't sure what he was leading up to.

"If you try to detach yourself from the personal aspect and look at it a little more scientifically, you really have no reason to feel discouraged. You have done all along what you were supposed to do." He pointed at my notebook. "You have all your observations written down, and you can round off your notes by drawing your own conclusions as to why everybody does things a certain way." He paused. "Actually the question of whether or not anyone follows your advice has nothing to do with your study. Can you understand that?"

I frowned. "No," I said. "I mean, the whole purpose for this project was to get everybody organized. Especially Vicki," I added.

Dad waved his hand. "Fine," he said. "I realize that. But we are now talking about the project as a study, which is what your teacher chose to call it. Just imagine for a second that you were doing this not with your own family but with, let's say, Jenny's family. Now, if they weren't cooperating, you probably wouldn't be so upset about it because you don't live with them anyway, so it doesn't really matter to you whether they are organized or not." He looked questioningly at me.

I was beginning to understand what he was getting at. "You mean I'm too personally involved," I said.

"That's right. You have to try to look at it more objectively."

I knew what he meant, but I still didn't like it. I sighed. "So what you want me to do is just ignore the fact that nobody really wants to try to change."

Dad smiled. "Yes and no," he said. "I still think it's a very worthwhile goal to try to get us all to change for the better, so by all means, don't give up on that. It's just that the outcome should not affect the quality of your project. Do you see what I mean? Besides, you haven't really given everybody a chance yet."

It finally began to make sense to me. But then I remembered my original problem. "So what do I do with Vicki?" I asked.

Dad sighed and thought for a second. Then he said, "I think that maybe you have to change *your* attitude toward her before she will change the way she acts."

"What do you mean?" I said, puzzled.

Dad cleared his throat and said, "You may not realize this, Karen, but lately you have been somewhat of a pest when it comes to dealing with your sister, and you can hardly expect her to be nice about it."

I felt my face turn red. "I don't know what you are talking about," I said defensively. "She's the one who's always mean."

Dad looked doubtful. "I think Vicki feels threatened by you in some ways," he said. "It hasn't been easy for her to get a new mother and two new sisters all of a sudden. You are a lot more self-confident than Vicki has ever been, and I think she resents that. She is at a difficult age anyway, and this past year hasn't been easy for her."

"You mean, you think it's been easy for me?" I said hotly. "At least Vicki still lives in her own house, while I had to move out of mine, and I had to give up my horse and my chickens and my rabbits." I blinked to keep my tears away. "Here I never have any privacy, and now I don't even have my own room, and I always have to wait to get into the bathroom and . . ." I felt a tear run down my cheek, and I couldn't help myself. I started crying.

Dad didn't say anything. He just waited until I calmed down.

"No, I don't think it's been easy for you either," he said kindly. "It's been difficult for all of us. Yet I think everything has gone smoother than I expected. Most families that move together because of remarriage have a lot more problems than we have had. And I have to give credit to you for the fact that there hasn't been a whole lot of dissension since you came here."

I wiped my face. "What do you mean?"

He smiled at me again. "I mean that you have adjusted beautifully, and you have done very little complaining, and you have acted very maturely. But," he pointed out, "I think because of that, Vicki resents you. So maybe what you need to do is go the extra mile and be especially nice to her. You may not have noticed, but Vicki has many good qualities that haven't been evident lately."

"Vicki is a lot prettier than I am," I said grudgingly.

Dad nodded. "She takes after her mother," he said. "Of course, I think she looks nicer without the makeup she insists on using." He sighed. "Or maybe I'm too old-fashioned."

He hadn't even seen what she looks like in school. I bit my lip. "No, I think you're right," I admitted. "And Vicki was nicer to me when we first moved here. It's just that she always says these mean things—"

"I don't think she really means what she says. It's a kind of defense that she puts up. I've been worried about her grades, however. A couple of years ago she had a B average, but nowadays it seems I should be grateful if she comes home with a D." Dad sighed and rubbed his chin. "But that might have nothing to do with my getting married. I guess she's at the age when boys are more important than grades."

He stared out the window for a while. Then he glanced at his watch and said, "Well, I guess I have to get some work done."

I got up from the floor and rubbed my legs, which had almost gone to sleep.

"I'll try to be nicer to Vicki," I said. "But it's not going to be easy."

"I know," Dad said. "But at least you know you are doing your best then even if she doesn't respond the way you want her to."

While I took the dogs for a walk, I thought about what Dad had said. I hated to admit it, but he was probably right about my having been a pest.

I sighed. It was just that Vicki always rubbed me the wrong way, and she always had these nasty remarks whenever I said something to her. Besides, she was older—it should be up to her to set a good example.

Then I remembered what Mom had told me once. In order to have friends, you yourself have to be a good friend.

And maybe I hadn't really tried to be friends with Vicki.

Chapter 10

During the next few days I really tried to be friendly with Vicki. Or at least I was never nasty back when she was nasty to me. It's hard to be really friendly with someone who treats you like poison.

When Grandma asked Vicki if she wanted to come along and visit the new people in the Patterson house, she said no, thanks, she didn't care whether we had new neighbors or not, and besides, she was busy. Then she lay down on the floor in our room and listened to records. I told Grandma I'd come with her instead since I was dying to meet the Millers anyway. Andy still didn't ride the bus, but he was in school every day. I had seen his brother, too, and he was just as good-looking as

Andy was. He seemed older than the rest of the seniors, although I guess he wasn't.

As boy-crazy as Vicki is, I couldn't understand why she didn't want to visit the Millers. It wasn't like her at all.

While I was brushing my hair and changing into my new sneakers, I said, "How come you don't want to go over and see Roger?"

Vicki didn't even open her eyes. "Roger who?"

"Roger Miller, of course," I said impatiently.

She sighed. "I have no idea what you are talking about. Now, can you be quiet so I can listen to the music?"

"You mean, you don't know who Roger Miller is?" I said incredulously.

"I already told you," she said coldly. "Now will you beat it?"

Ignoring that, I said, "For your information, Roger Miller is the new tall, blond, good-looking guy in the senior class who just moved to town. And the Millers bought the Pattersons' house and they used to live in Texas and Roger has a brother who is in my class and his name is Andy." I stopped to catch my breath.

But Vicki was already sitting up straight with her mouth open. "You mean, that's Roger Miller?" she exclaimed. "The guy with the brown suede blazer?"

I nodded. "That's the one," I said.

Vicki kept on staring at me. "But I've never seen him on our bus."

"Of course you haven't," I explained. "He has his own car. Andy doesn't ride the bus either."

Vicki was already over by the mirror, pulling a comb through her hair. "Tell Grandma I'll be ready in five minutes," she said.

I sat down on her bed and finished tying my shoelaces. "You already told her you weren't going," I said mildly. "I'm going with her."

Vicki pretended she didn't hear me. She looked at me through the mirror. "Can you find my pink velour sweater? It's in the dresser."

I was just going to say something sarcastic when I remembered that I was supposed to be nice to her. Instead, I started pulling out the drawers, which was easier said than done. They were so jammed with clothes that were just thrown in that they could barely be opened. Naturally I didn't find her sweater.

"It's not here," I said.

"Then look in the closet." Now she was putting on eye shadow.

I opened the closet door. I guess it was some sign of progress that it could still be shut, but otherwise the closet was back in the same condition as it was before she had cleaned it out.

I had no idea whether the sweater was there or not. It was probably easier to find a needle in a haystack.

"If you ever want to get your clothes organized, I'll help you," I offered. "Then it will be easier for you to find things." I had already resigned myself to the fact that I wasn't going to the Millers', and I thought I'd take a chance and put in a plug for my project.

Vicki walked over to the closet, and without hesitating, she pulled her arm through the mess and produced the pink sweater. It was like someone pulling a white rabbit out of a hat.

"You'd better stay out of my stuff," she said threateningly. She pulled the sweater over her head, and grabbing her shoes, she went over to the door. "I'll tell what's-his-name you said hello," she said.

When she shut the door behind her, I yelled, "Andy. His name is Andy." I kicked off my sneakers again and threw them in the corner. Then I went over and picked them up and put them by my bed.

Lord Nelson was sleeping on the floor on Arthur's blanket. I woke him up, and after I had got my old sneakers on again, we went outside. Arthur was lying in the front yard, watching Ryan and Meghan playing with their Tonka trucks.

Lord Nelson and I crossed the road and continued along the side of the wheat field. I always take a walk when I am mad. It helps me calm down. We walked around almost the whole field, and then we cut through the woods until we came back to the road again before heading home.

I decided I'd invite Andy to come over to our house tomorrow. And if he thought it would be embarrassing to visit a girl, maybe I could get Marcus to ask him.

When I got back to the house, I was in a good mood again. I'd forgotten to check on Ryan after school, so I went into the kitchen. The garbage was gone. So far Ryan had done pretty well, although what he called making a bed wasn't exactly what I called making a bed. I'd decided not to say anything, though. After all, he was only six, and Marcus's bed didn't look much better either.

There were only two toys on the hall floor, and I picked those up. I checked under the boys' beds. There were a few dirty clothes there, but not very many. Since it was already Friday and they hadn't started cleaning their room yet, that was a positive sign.

I guessed I should be grateful for any little step in the right direction, even though I had a feeling things would slide back to what they had been before too long.

I peeked into Meghan's room, too, although I really hadn't involved her in my project. She is pretty neat for her age.

Last, I made sure all my signs were still up, although I didn't think anyone was paying attention to them anymore. Vicki had been on the phone as much as ever this week, and when she wasn't on the phone, she was in the bathroom.

Mom was in the living room, writing a letter. She looked up when I came in. "I thought you went with Grandma," she said.

I shook my head. "I changed my mind. Vicki went instead." I really didn't feel like explaining why, so I changed the subject. "What's for dinner?"

Mom was reading through her letter. She frowned. "We're having leftovers." Then she said, "I'm writing to Grandmother. Is there anything you want me to say?"

I thought about it for a moment. "Hmmm, I don't think so. I wrote her a letter last week." I picked up one of the cats, who was trying to climb up my leg. "Ask her when she is coming here."

"Oh, I guess I forgot to tell you. She called yesterday while you were at school. She said she'll be here for Thanksgiving."

"*Thanksgiving?* But that's a whole month away. I thought she was going to come as soon as you had the baby."

Mom looked at me. "The baby isn't due until next week, and then Thanksgiving is only three weeks away. I think that will be soon enough. Besides, I think Grandmother is busy right now." She looked mysterious.

"Busy with what?" My grandmother, who lives in California, is all by herself, and she doesn't work. She is very active and belongs to a lot of clubs and things like that. She also plays golf, and every summer she flies to Sweden to see her relatives. She was born in Sweden and came over here when she was very young.

Mom smiled. "She has a boyfriend. And from what I can tell, it sounds very serious."

I stared at her. "You mean, she is getting married?"

Mom shrugged. "I wouldn't be surprised if she did. In fact, I hope she will. It's been almost eight years since my father died, and I'd hate to see her alone for the rest of her life. She's only fifty-seven."

"She could come and live with us," I said.

Mom got up from her chair and went over to the window. I knew she was looking to see if Dad was coming. "That's not what I was talking about," she said. "Grandmother needs a companion. Someone she can fuss over and cook for and do things with." She walked to the sofa and sat down. "You know she wouldn't be happy living here. Remember, even when it was just you and I, she didn't want to come stay. It's too quiet for her up here."

I knew. We tried for years to get Grandmother to come live with us, but she always got restless after visiting for a few weeks.

I still couldn't get over that she might get married, though. "What kind of guy is she seeing?" I asked.

"A very nice man, according to Grandmother. He is a retired businessman, sixty-two years old, has three children, who are all married, and seven grandchildren."

"Do you think I could be a bridesmaid again?" I said hopefully. "I still have my dress."

Mom laughed. "I doubt that they will have a big wedding, honey. Probably a small ceremony. And anyway, I think such plans are premature. All she said when she called was that she has known him for several months and that they see each other practically every day."

Is he going to come here for Thanksgiving, too?"

Mom looked surprised. "Not that I know of," she said. "However, if they are still seeing each other, we might ask if she would like to bring him along."

I could hear Dad's truck outside. Mom went outside to greet him, and I went back upstairs. I wondered what I was supposed to call Grandmother's friend if they did get married. I guessed he would be my grandfather, or would he be my stepgrandfather?

I sighed. When people remarried, it sure complicated things. But it would be nice to have a grandfather. I already had two grandmothers, but I have never had a grandfather.

Chapter 11

It was one of those beautiful fall days when you just can't stay indoors. Andrea Baxter, who is in my class, had been over all morning, and she and I had run the sixty-yard distance that Dad marked off for us. We timed each other with Mom's stopwatch.

The first time I was three seconds faster than Andrea, but the last lap I was way behind. I think Andrea has more endurance because she takes gymnastics twice a week. Maybe I should start doing that, too.

Andrea's mother picked her up after lunch, and at three o'clock all of us kids piled into the back of our truck. We were going down to the river for a picnic dinner. Dad was driving, and Mom and Grandma were riding up front with him.

The picnic was Mom's idea. She said we might not

have many more days like this before winter. Besides, she wanted to get out of the house for a while.

She is really getting enormous, and even Dad said that if he didn't know better, he'd say she must be expecting twins. The baby is due any day now, and Dad doesn't want Mom to take walks by herself just in case she should fall.

The river is about four miles away from our house, going north. It's not much of a river actually, but it's better than nothing. During the summer months you can walk across and the water doesn't reach any higher than your waist. Right now it's deeper than that, of course, because we've had a lot of rain lately.

Both sides of the river are heavily wooded, but there are a couple of clearings that are pretty nice. That's usually where we go because we can play ball and things like that there.

When we came down to the river, the boys took off their shoes and socks and started chasing each other in the water. I told them they were crazy. The water was freezing.

After a while Lord Nelson joined the boys, and I played hide-and-seek with Meghan. Vicki finished the book she had been reading and disappeared behind the trees. Mom and Grandma started putting out the food.

Dad, who had been turning over rocks, looking for worms, said, "Why don't you wait with dinner until I've caught some fish? It won't take long."

Grandma eyed him doubtfully. "Probably long enough for the rest of the food to go bad," she said.

Dad looked hurt. "I bet I'll catch at least two within half an hour."

"How much?" Grandma said promptly.

"Ten dollars."

"It's a bet." She put the food that wasn't covered back in the box so the dogs wouldn't get at it.

"What are you going to do with the money?" I asked her.

Grandma waited until Dad was out of hearing distance before she answered. She looked smug. "I'll buy him a book about fishing for Christmas," she said.

I giggled. "What if he wins?"

Grandma looked confident. "He hasn't yet," she said. "We do this at least twice a year. He never learns. Easiest money I ever make." She grabbed Arthur by the collar and dragged him away from the food.

Lord Nelson was still out in the water, so I tried to get Arthur to go with me for a walk. He wouldn't come, of course. He knew who was in charge of the food, and he was sticking to Grandma like glue.

Grandma is really bad about giving Arthur treats, and right now he is at least ten pounds overweight. Mom has asked her not to feed Arthur any more scraps, but Grandma defends herself by saying that he is looking weak and listless and needs to build up his strength. She doesn't understand that Arthur is just putting on an act for her.

I've seen him myself, begging for food when Grandma is in the kitchen. He stands in the doorway and kind of leans against the doorframe as if he had trouble keeping himself up. His head is about six inches from the floor, and his tongue is hanging out. Every now and then he sighs really loud. It's heartbreaking to watch him. Mom says that Arthur should be nominated for an Oscar for best acting performance.

Mom and Meghan were watching Dad fish, so finally I went for a walk by myself.

There is a very narrow path that winds through the

trees along the riverbank. It's just right for hiking because on and off you can see the water, and the ground is
covered with a thick layer of pine needles which makes it
feel as if you were walking on a very soft carpet.

I had walked for maybe ten minutes when I ran into
Vicki. Literally. I had my eyes on the ground, and my
mind was really far away, so I didn't even see her. I guess
she wasn't watching either because we suddenly col-
lided, and I slipped on the pine needles and sat down
smack on my bottom.

I must have looked pretty funny because Vicki started
laughing. "You look like someone in those old gag mov-
ies," she said.

I made a face and got back up on my feet. "Ha-ha," I
said coolly. My bottom really hurt.

"Is everybody eating?" Vicki asked.

I shook my head and brushed the pine needles off my
pants. "Dad made a bet with Grandma that he'd catch at
least two fish in half an hour." I checked my watch.
"We'd better get back. Time is almost up."

Vicki suppressed a smile. "Dad never catches anything," she commented. "He always makes bets with
Grandma, and he always loses."

We started walking back. The sun was filtering down
through the trees, casting an everchanging pattern on
the ground. It was getting warm, and I pushed up the
sleeves of my sweater.

"I wonder how long this weather is going to last. It's
too good to be true. This time last year we already had
snow."

"Please don't mention the word." Vicki shuddered. "I
hate snow. Sometimes I wish we lived somewhere else
where we'd have more summer and less winter."

"Mom grew up in California, but she likes it better up

here," I said. Then I thought of something. "Maybe you could visit my grandmother down there sometimes."

Vicki's face lit up. "You think I could? I mean, really? Do you think you could ask her?"

"She'll be here for Thanksgiving. You can ask her yourself then. I'm sure she'd love to have you. When I visit her, she always takes me to fashion shows and art galleries and all kinds of neat places."

Vicki's face lost her pleased expression. "I wish I could go during Christmas vacation, but I bet Dad won't let me," she said gloomily. "Just because of my grades."

"If you get your grades up, maybe you can go next summer."

She stuck her hands in her jeans pockets. "That's almost a year away."

"Or maybe during spring break," I added.

It suddenly dawned on me that for the first time in months Vicki and I were having a perfectly normal conversation. I'd almost forgotten how nice it could be.

I guess Dad was right when he said it was partly my fault that Vicki was so nasty. Lately I had really made an effort to be nice to her.

Now I took a deep breath and said, "I'm sorry if I bugged you too much with my project. I . . . uh . . . I'm supposed to include everybody in the family. That's why I had to ask all those questions." I thought I'd better not tell her she was the reason I had started the project in the first place.

Vicki pulled the ribbon out of her hair so it fell loosely over her shoulders. She has the most beautiful blond hair I've ever seen. It's even prettier than Mom's, and it has just a touch of curl to it. Mom's is absolutely straight.

"It's okay," she said finally.

"It's harder to think of a decent project," I explained.

"And once I've started, I have to finish it whether I like it or not."

"I said it's okay," Vicki repeated. "Just . . . I just don't want to hear any more about it."

We walked on in silence. Suddenly she said, "I guess what bugs me is the fact that I have to share my room."

"So how do you think I like it?" I asked. "I didn't like giving up my privacy either. I've always had my own room. Don't you wish we had a bigger house? Right this minute, I mean?" I sighed wistfully.

"Well, we don't, so I guess we'll have to do the best with what we have," Vicki said reasonably.

"I'll stay out of your way," I promised.

Grandma was putting the food out again, and Dad looked sheepish when we asked him where the fish was. Grandma pulled the ten-dollar bill out of her pocket and waved it in the air.

"He says they don't bite because the weather is too nice," she said. "Remind me that next time we go on a picnic we'll pick a rainy day."

I was famished, and as usual I ate too much. Mom says she is hoping that one of these days I'll wise up and stop stuffing myself, but I don't think I ever will. Everything looks so good, and I always think I'm able to eat more than I really can.

Fortunately I stay skinny no matter what. I know that really bothers Vicki because she gains a pound when she has an extra sandwich at night. She is forever dieting to keep her weight down.

Mom says I'll change when I get older and more developed. I guess when that day comes, I'll be the fattest girl in school.

After the food had been put away, we played catch for a while, and then we jumped on the rocks that were out in the water. We were supposed to jump from one rock to the next without getting wet because we all had our sneakers on. It worked all right until Marcus lost his balance and fell in. Then Dad said it was time go home.

He made Marcus take off his wet jeans so he wouldn't catch pneumonia. There was an old blanket in the truck that Marcus had to wrap himself in. He was so mad he didn't say a word the whole trip back.

Vicki and I played a game of chess before we went to bed. We hadn't done that since the beginning of summer. She won, but I didn't mind. I could have beaten her, but she is such a sore loser I thought I'd make the sacrifice to stay on her good side.

It sure feels a lot nicer to share a room with a sister who acts like a human being instead of your number one enemy.

Just before I went to sleep, I thought that maybe Vicki felt the same way.

Chapter 12

On Monday morning Mr. Campbell told me he wanted my finished project report by the end of the week, Thursday if possible.

When I made a face, he said, "There is no need to look so unhappy. Things have been going all right, haven't they?"

I sighed and chewed on my hair. Then I decided to tell him the truth, which was that hardly anything had changed at home. When I was done, he said, "Well, then that's your conclusion."

I told him about my conversation with Dad. "Vicki is a lot nicer now," I said, "because I'm nicer to her. But she isn't any more organized than she was before. And she still spends half her life in the bathroom. She isn't as mean as before, but . . ." I left the sentence unfinished.

Mr. Campbell nodded encouragingly. "At least you've

gotten something positive out of your project. That's great. And maybe you have sown a few seeds."

"What do you mean?" I asked.

"You have made them all aware of the fact that they are not functioning as effectively as they should. Maybe someday they'll *really* get motivated enough to want to change."

"Oh, yeah?" I said, unconvinced. I was silent for a moment, and then I said, "I guess I didn't pick a very good project, that's all."

Mr. Campbell wiped the chalk off his hands. "On the contrary," he said. "I think it was an excellent choice. Your father was right when he said that the way your family responded to your efforts to change them had nothing to do with the quality of your project.

"It's not how people react that counts. It's how well you have observed their reaction, regardless of whether it's good or bad. And from what I've heard so far, you've done a great job." He patted my shoulder. "I'm looking forward to seeing the finished report."

I spent the rest of the day worrying about my report, and I hardly ate anything at lunchtime. I had made sandwiches to bring to school, but as usual I'd left them in the refrigerator, so I had to use my lunch ticket.

Dad pays for a ten-day ticket each month; that means half the time we have to bring cold lunches. I try to save my tickets for those days when the cafeteria serves food I really like, but usually I've used them all up by the twentieth or so.

Today we had a ham sandwich with sauerkraut. It tasted horrible. I gave my sandwich to Chris. He is in my class, and he eats anything. It shows, too. He must weigh about two hundred pounds. When he walks, his bottom wobbles. It's disgusting.

Mom told me not to pick on him because maybe he has a thyroid problem or something like that which makes him gain weight. I told her I don't pick on him, I just think he looks disgusting. Then she said that's exactly what she was talking about. I shouldn't go around and tell people he looks disgusting.

Sometimes Mom and I have trouble communicating.

I was brooding over my project all the way home, and I barely answered when Jenny tried to talk to me. Finally she gave up and returned to her comic book.

When we came home, Meghan went to look for Mom. I checked the kitchen for our after-school snack, but there was none. Ryan went straight to the TV as usual without even taking off his coat. If he could, Ryan would spend all his waking hours in front of the television.

Vicki was already upstairs, and Marcus had stayed in town with his best friend. Nobody seemed to mind that there was no snack out except me.

When Meghan came down the stairs again, I said, "Where's Mom?"

She shrugged. "I don't know." Then she added, "Grandma isn't home either."

"Oh," I said, "they must have gone shopping."

Mom can't get in behind the wheel anymore, so whenever she has to go to town, Grandma has to drive her.

I took an apple from the basket in the kitchen. My stomach felt funny. I wasn't sure whether it was because I was hungry or because I was worrying about my project. It was probably both.

I was just going upstairs when the phone rang. It was Grandma.

"Is that you, Karen?" she asked.

"Yes, Grandma. Where are you? Is Mom with you? What are we supposed to have for a snack?"

Grandma's voice sounded far away. "I'm at the hospital, honey. Your mother had some labor pains, and I had to drive her in. Now your father is on his way here, so I'm leaving as soon as he arrives. I should be home in half an hour."

It took a while for the information to sink in. Then I yelled, "Hospital! Labor pains! You mean, Mom is having her baby?"

I almost ripped the phone off the wall in my excitement. "Has he come yet? Grandma, is Mom okay? Is it a boy or a girl? Can we come see him? When is Mom coming home?" I hadn't even noticed Ryan coming into the kitchen.

He took the receiver out of my hand. "Grandma," he shouted, "are you bringing the baby home?"

Meghan was pulling at my shirt, wondering what was going on. I grabbed her and danced around the kitchen. "Mom's having a baby. Mom's having a baby," I sang.

Then Vicki came downstairs, and I said breathlessly, "Grandma is on the phone and Mom's having the baby and she'll be home in half an hour."

Vicki stared at me as if she thought I'd gone crazy. "If Mom is having the baby, she'll hardly be home in half an hour," she said dryly.

I threw up my arms. "Not Mom," I said impatiently. "Grandma will be home in half an hour. She's at the hospital now, and she'll leave as soon as Dad gets there."

Without another word Vicki grabbed the phone away from Ryan.

"I bet it's a girl," I said. "I just *know* it is."

"Mom said I can help give the baby her bath," Meghan announced importantly. "I bet she won't let anybody else do it."

"How do you know it's a girl?" Ryan said in disgust.

"It might be a boy. It'd better be a boy," he added darkly, "or I'm moving out. There are too many girls in this house already."

"Did Grandma say?" I asked. "Did she say what it was?" I gave Ryan a nudge. "Did you ask?"

"No, I didn't ask." Ryan stuck his tongue out. "I asked if I could watch *The Six Million Dollar Man* until she came home, that's what I asked."

That really made me mad. "You mean, that's all you thought about?" I shouted. "Your dumb television programs? Don't you even care about the baby?"

"I didn't ask for it, did I?" Ryan's face was red, and he stared angrily at me. "If you want to know, I think we have enough kids already, and if . . ."

Nobody had noticed that Vicki was finished with the phone call. Meghan started yelling back at Ryan, and I yelled at both of them.

Vicki grabbed them by the arms and shook them. "Cut it out, you two. What's the matter with you guys? Why can't you behave?" Looking at me, she continued. "Grandma said it was just a false alarm. Mom isn't having the baby yet. But the doctor said she'd better stay at the hospital overnight."

"Is Dad going to stay, too?" I asked.

Vicki shook her head. "Of course not. Grandma said he'll be home later on." She looked from Ryan to Meghan. "And you two had better behave or I'm going to tell Dad when he comes back.

"Oh, yes," she added. "I'd better get the casserole out of the freezer before I forget or we won't have any dinner."

I trailed behind her into the utility room. "If Mom has to stay in the hospital tomorrow, too, can I go see her?" Suddenly I was scared. Mom had never had a baby before, and maybe something was terribly wrong and Grandma didn't tell us. "How come she started having the baby and then she didn't?"

Vicki turned around. It must have shown on my face how worried I was, for she said in a kind voice, "Of course, she didn't start having the baby. She just had a few pains that stopped after they got to the hospital. That's all. Everybody who is going to have a baby soon has to go through that."

"Oh," I said. I already felt much better. "Do you think we can go see her tommorrow?"

"She'll probably be home, but if she isn't, you can't visit her anyway. They won't let anybody in under sixteen."

I'd never heard of anything so dumb. "But she's my mother!" I exclaimed. "You mean, I can't go see my own mother?"

I followed Vicki back to the kitchen.

"It's hospital policy," she said patiently. "They won't let children into the maternity ward. But," she added, "you can see the baby through the window."

At eight I took Lord Nelson with me and went for a long walk. When I came home again, Dad was just driving up in the yard.

I waited for him to get out of the car, and then I said, "How is Mom? Is she coming home tomorrow?"

Dad put his arm around me as we walked up to the house. "She's fine and probably asleep by now. If nothing happens before morning, she'll be home again tomorrow." He smiled reassuringly. "There is nothing to worry about, believe me. I know this is your mother's first baby, but I've had three before, so I know everything is proceeding normally."

"You have had three babies before?"

Dad raised his eyebrows. "Of course. Vicki, Marcus, and Ryan."

I giggled. "I didn't know you had them, Dad," I said. "I thought it was your wife who had them."

Dad laughed. Then he squeezed my shoulder. "Of course it was. But believe me, sometimes it's just as agonizing for the father when the baby is born."

I opened the front door. "Hah," I said. "Try to tell Mom that."

I read until past midnight because I couldn't sleep. Usually Vicki complains when I have the light on when she wants to sleep, but this time she didn't say a word.

Dad called the hospital early next morning and was told that the doctor wanted Mom to stay until the baby was born. Just in case.

"Just in case what?" I said.

"Just in case it comes early," Dad explained.

"Can I stay home from school today?"

Dad looked surprised. "Why?" he asked. "Don't you feel well?"

I was trying to cram my sneakers into my backpack, but I had too many books there already. Instead, I tied the shoelaces to the strap.

"Of course, I'm feeling well," I said. "I just want to be home in case the baby comes, that's all."

"You'll hear about it soon enough after school."

"Won't the hospital call and tell you?"

"I certainly hope so."

"Then can't you call me at school?"

"You'll find out when you come home."

I gave him a pleading look. "Please?" I said. "I can't stand waiting all day without knowing."

Dad sighed. "Okay," he said, relenting. "I promise I'll call the school and leave a message. How's that?"

I gave him a quick hug. "Thanks, Dad. You're the greatest. After all," I pointed out, "this is my very first baby."

I said, "Who knows? Maybe the baby will grow up to be a famous scientist. Or the first woman president. Or a famous . . . whatever."

Dad shook his head. "We'll worry about that later. I'm afraid he or she will start out like the rest of you."

"What do you mean?"

"I mean that for the next eighteen years he'll try to drive his parents up the wall." Dad's eyes twinkled.

"You mean, the way the boys do? But maybe the baby will be a girl. Girls are easier to raise, aren't they?"

"They are?" He looked doubtful.

"Of course they are," I said. "We never do any of the bad stuff boys do. And we have more common sense."

"Hmmm," Dad said. "I think I'll have to take the fifth on that one."

I looked puzzled. "Take what?"

"The Fifth Amendment." Dad grinned. "That means I claim the right to refuse to answer any questions that might incriminate me."

He picked up his briefcase and started for the door.

"I didn't know you were so chicken," I said. Walking back to the kitchen, I sang, "Daddy is chicken, Daddy is chicken . . ."

He was still laughing when he slammed the door behind him.

Chapter 13

As soon as I arrived at school, I went to the office and told Mrs. Gonzalez that I might be getting a phone call.

"Mom is about to have a baby," I said, "so be sure and tell me if Dad calls."

"I promise," Mrs. G. said solemnly. "Is it going to be a boy or a girl?"

"I wish I knew. I hope it will be a girl. Mom says she'll take whatever comes, of course."

Mrs. G. folded her arms and leaned back in her chair. "You mean your mother hasn't taken the coffee test?"

"The coffee test?" I stared at her. "What's that?"

Shaking her head, Mrs. G. said, "You mean, you don't know about the coffee test? It's the only sure way to find out ahead of time whether it's going to be a boy or a girl." She nodded her head solemnly. "That's how my mother knew about me before I was born."

"I've never heard of it," I said skeptically.

"In Puerto Rico everyone who is pregnant takes the coffee test. That way they don't have to worry about boys' names when it's going to be a girl and vice versa."

I thought that what she said made sense. "How do you do it?" I asked.

Mrs. Gonzalez leaned forward and said, "You make a fresh pot of coffee, really black and strong. Then you drink two cups, one after another as quickly as you can. No sugar, no cream, just coffee. Oh, yes, you must not eat or drink anything else for six hours before you drink the coffee." She nodded vigorously. "My mother always had the coffee in the morning."

"And then what?" I asked.

"Then you wait five minutes. If you feel sick, it's going to be a girl. If you feel fine, it's a boy."

I thought about it for a moment. At least it sounded simple enough. "How do you know it really works?" I said.

"It works." Mrs. Gonzalez put a pencil in the electric sharpener. It started buzzing. "My mother did it every time she was expecting, and it worked every time."

"How many children did your mother have?"

Just then the phone rang. Mrs. Gonzalez put her hand on the receiver and said to me, "She had thirteen. Four boys and nine girls."

I was still thinking about what she had said when I walked into my classroom. How could anybody live with twelve sisters and brothers? And I had thought six was a lot.

I guess my mind wasn't on my schoolwork that day because twice Miss Stevens had to raise her voice and repeat the question to get my attention, and when Andy talked to me during recess, I just stared dumbly at him.

"Did you say something?" I asked.

He leaned against the wall and put his hands in his pocket. "I asked if you and Vicki would like a ride home after school. My brother has his car today."

"I guess so," I said. "But I'll have to ask Vicki."

"Roger is asking her."

"Oh," I said. Normally I'd be in seventh heaven to get an invitation like that, but today all I could think of was Mom.

"Of course, I might have to go to the hospital after school," I informed him. I told him why. "But if I don't, I'd love to ride with you."

"Gee, that's neat," Andy said. "I bet you're excited." Just then the bell rang. "Let me know by three o'clock," he said over his shoulder.

I hurried downstairs to my class, and I even managed to get a few math problems done before school was out. When I was ready to leave, I went up to Mr. Campbell and said, "Can I hand in my report on Monday instead of tomorrow?"

"Sure. No problem. I hear you're getting the new addition to your family today."

"How did you know?" I asked in surprise.

He pointed upward. "A little bird told me."

I giggled. I knew he meant Mrs. G. "You mean Big Bird?" I said. Then I clamped my hand over my mouth. It had slipped out before I had time to think. I hoped Mr. Campbell didn't think I had meant to be rude. But when I looked at him, he was smiling.

"You can tell me all about it tomorrow," he said.

"Did you know that Mrs. Gonzalez's mother had thirteen children?" I asked. "I guess I shouldn't complain.

Even with the baby there will be only six of us."

"Maybe your mother will have triplets," he said gravely.

I suppressed a giggle. "Have you ever heard of the coffee test?"

He looked puzzled. "No. Should I?"

"Your wife should."

Then I remembered that Andy was waiting for me. I'd better leave, or they might think I'd gone with the bus.

"Ask Mrs. Gonzalez," I said. "She can tell you all about it." I opened the door.

"I will. Good-bye, Karen."

"Bye, Mr. Campbell. See you tomorrow."

Chapter 14

The baby was born the next day at 2:45 P.M. It was a boy. When we came home from school, Grandma was still talking to Dad on the phone. He had been at the hospital all day.

"Your mother is fine, the baby is fine, and we'll all go in and see him after dinner," Grandma said after she had hung up.

"After dinner!" I exclaimed. "Why do we have to wait until after dinner? Why can't we go now?"

"After dinner, Grandma repeated. "That will give your mother time to get some rest."

I was too excited to do homework, so first I called

Jenny and gave her the big news, and then I called Grandmother in California.

"How much does he weigh?" Grandmother asked.

"Eight pounds and four ounces," I said proudly. "And he has lots of black hair."

"Does he look like me?" she wanted to know.

"How do I know?" I said. "I haven't seen him yet. We're going in after dinner. Do you want me to call you when we come back?"

She thought for a moment. "No, darling. I'll call you instead. And I'll call your mother at the hospital, too. By the way, does my grandson have a name?"

"Of course. His name is Jonathan. Jonathan Matthew Carlson." Suddenly I remembered something. "Are you going to bring your boyfriend when you visit us for Thanksgiving?"

There was silence at the other end. Then she said, "My what?"

"Your boyfriend. Mom told me all about him."

She coughed. "I bet she did," she said dryly.

"You haven't split up, have you? He sounded nice to me."

After another silence Grandmother said, "I never thought I'd have to discuss my men friends with my granddaughter. But since you insist. No, we haven't split up, and yes, he is a very nice man, and we spend a lot of time together. However, we are not going to get married, and we are not engaged, and he is not coming with me." She paused. "Does that satisfy your curiosity?"

I moved the receiver to my other ear. "I guess so," I said. "I still would like to meet him though. I'd hate to see you getting involved with someone who doesn't deserve you."

"Don't worry, darling." She sounded amused. "I'm perfectly capable of taking care of myself."

"I hope so," I said doubtfully. "Do you have a picture of him? I"d still like to see what he looks like. Is he taller than you are?"

Grandmother started laughing. "I can see now what you put your poor mother's friends through. No wonder none of them wanted to marry her."

She was talking about the summer before last, when Mom still hadn't met Dad and I spent months trying to find her a husband.

"I was only trying to help," I said. "Most children probably don't care who their grandmother goes out with."

She laughed again. "I'm sure you're right. And I do appreciate your concern, darling. When he proposes, I promise you'll be the first one to know."

"Really? Thanks, Grandmother. You'd better not forget."

There were seven newborn babies in that room at the hospital, but my brother was the cutest of them all. None of the others had even half as much hair as he did.

"How come he is so red?" Ryan asked suspiciously. "He looks weird."

Vicki gave him a superior look. "All babies are red," she said. "He'll look better tomorrow."

"How do you know?"

"You'll see."

"What if he doesn't?" Ryan persisted.

"Don't worry, he will."

"How do *you* know? You never had a baby."

Marcus gave Ryan a push. "Ha-ha," he said. "You were just as red when *you* were born. Even I remember that."

Ryan turned around angrily. "I wasn't either."

"You were, too."

"I was not. And you can't—"

Fortunately Dad came right then or I guess the boys would have started fighting. Grandma had gone in to see Mom.

"Well, what do you think?" Dad asked proudly.

Meghan stood with her face pressed against the window while the nurse was holding Jonathan so we could see him close up. "Can I take him home?" she asked wistfully.

Everybody laughed, and Dad said, "Not yet. Mom will bring him the day after tomorrow."

Saturday morning we all helped get the house clean for Mom's return. Dad was going in to get her and Jonathan at noon.

Vicki was supposed to straighten up the family room before I vacuumed, but when I looked for her, she had locked herself in the bathroom.

When she still hadn't come out after twenty minutes, I banged on the door. "Hurry up," I said. "I can't vacuum until you have picked up the mess on the floor."

While I was waiting, I went into my old room, which now was the nursery. Mom had bought a crib with matching dresser, and Grandma had made a new skirt for Ryan's old bassinet. The green rug had been replaced by an oval shag carpet in two shades of blue. It looked really nice.

I came back out in the hall just as the doorbell rang. I wondered who it could be. I hoped it wasn't Mrs. Olson because she usually stays forever and talks and talks.

But it wasn't Mrs. Olson. It was Roger and Andy.

"Hi," I said. I certainly hadn't expected to see them.

"Hi." Roger was holding a large round plastic container. "Mom sent us over with this. She heard your mother is coming home today."

He made no attempt to give it to me, so I stepped aside and said, "Why don't you come in? I'll go get Grandma."

When I returned from the kitchen, Roger and Andy were in the living room. Meghan, who was supposed to be dusting, was trying to get a peek at what was in the container.

"I bet it's a cake," she said.

Andy shook his head. "It's peach pie. Two of them."

Grandma came and took the pies. She said it was very thoughtful of Mrs. Miller and that she'd call and thank her. After she had left, I said, "Do you want to see the nursery?"

They looked at each other. Then Andy said politely, "Sure."

Neither of them looked very enthusiastic, and I already wished I hadn't asked. I guess boys aren't that interested in babies.

When we passed the kitchen, Grandma asked, "Have you and Vicki finished cleaning the family room?"

"She hasn't even started," I said self-righteously. "Of course, I can't vacuum until she's done. She has been in the bathroom for the past half hour."

Grandma shook her head wearily. When we went into the nursery, I heard her knock on the bathroom door. I didn't hear what she said, but Vicki yelled back, "Why don't you all leave me alone? I'm tired of being pushed around all the time."

Grandma said something again, and Vicki answered, "Tell Miss Goody-Goody to get off my back and mind her own business instead."

Roger and Andy could hear every word, of course. It was pretty embarrassing. We stood in the nursery, looking around. Finally Roger said, "That looks pretty neat." I could tell he was uncomfortable. We returned to the living room in silence.

"Well," Roger said, "I guess we'd better leave." He zipped up his Windbreaker.

"Oh, you don't have to go," I said quickly.

"I thought you had to clean the family room," Andy reminded me.

I shrugged. "I can't vacuum until Vicki is done with her part."

We all walked out to the hall. Roger said, "Does Vicki always act like that?"

"Hah!" I exclaimed. "That was nothing. You should hear some of the things she says to me." Belatedly I remembered that I was supposed to be nice to her. "But that's only when she's in a bad mood, of course. Most of the time she's okay."

Dad came out of the study to say hello to the boys. Five seconds later Vicki came out of the bathroom. She must have heard Dad's voice and figured that she'd better not press her luck.

When she saw Roger, she lit up like a Christmas tree. "Oh, hi there," she said. "I didn't know you were here. Did you just come?"

"They're just leaving," I said with satisfaction. "Too bad you were so busy. They've been here for quite a while."

Vicki gave me a furious glare. "Why didn't you tell me?" she asked, trying to control her temper.

Roger and Andy walked outside, still talking to Dad. "Thanks again for the pies," I called after them. "See you Monday." Then I slammed the door shut.

"Why didn't you tell me they were here?" Vicki muttered. "You know I would have come out."

I raised my eyebrows. "No, I didn't know," I said innocently. "I tried to get you out, and so did Grandma." I added meaningfully, "We *all* heard how tired you were of being pushed around."

Vicki's face turned red, and she turned around and ran upstairs. She must have realized that Roger and Andy had heard her yelling at Grandma. For a moment I felt sorry for her, but then I thought it served her right. Maybe next time she'd think twice before she opened her mouth to be rude.

When Dad came back in, he said, "I'm leaving for the hospital now. Are you all done with the housecleaning?"

I opened my mouth to tell on Vicki, but I shut it again. It was tempting but just because she was back to her old nasty ways didn't mean that I had to lower myself. "Just about," I said. "We'll be done before you get back."

"Great." He opened the closet door and took out his jacket. "See you in a little while."

"Make sure you get the right baby," I cautioned him. "I read in a magazine that sometimes the hospitals get them mixed up."

Dad pretended to look indifferent. "So what?" he said. "A baby is a baby. They all are pretty much the same. Besides, your mother probably has the right one ready to go."

I thought of how disorganized Mom is. "Don't bet on it," I warned. "You'd better make sure yourself. Remember that ours is the one with the most hair."

Chapter 15

"Karen."

"Yes."

"Are you sleeping?"

"No." I had been. Almost. It was past eleven, and I had been up since six o'clock. That's when Jonathan woke me up. I guess it will take awhile to get used to having a baby in the house.

"Has Roger said anything about me?" Vicki's voice was muffled.

I rolled over and hugged my pillow. "What do you mean?"

"Today, when you and Roger were out in the garage getting apples, what did you talk about?"

I could hear her moving around in the dark. Propping myself up on one elbow, I said, "Nothing much. He asked how many apple trees we had, and I told him we had four. Then I asked him if he was going to the high school dance the week after next, and he said he might."

After a moment's silence Vicki said, "Did he say who he was going with?"

I sighed impatiently. "Of course not. Maybe he isn't going at all."

"You mean you didn't even ask who he was going with?"

"No, I didn't."

Vicki didn't say anything more, and I lay back in my bed again. Now I was wide-awake. I hoped I wouldn't be too tired in the morning.

Roger and Andy and their parents had stopped by in the morning on their way home from church to have a look at the baby. Mom had invited them in for coffee, and they ended up staying for almost an hour.

Before the Millers left, Dad asked me to show Roger where the apples were in the garage because we were giving them a couple of boxes. This year we had a bumper crop, and there was no way we could ever eat all of it.

My eyes were adjusting to the dark, and through a peephole in my bookcase I could see Vicki sitting up in her bed.

"Why don't you go to sleep?" I suggested, yawning. "Remember we have school tomorrow."

Vicki didn't move, and finally I lay down and pulled the blanket over my head. I was just drifting back into unconsciousness when she said, "Do you think Roger likes me?" Without waiting for an answer she continued. "Sometimes I think he does, but then sometimes he completely ignores me. Like today. First he came into the kitchen to say hello, but then he wouldn't even stay and talk." Her voice was bitter. "You'd think I was contagious or something."

I covered my head with my pillow, so I wouldn't have to listen; but she went on and on, and even though I couldn't hear what she was saying, it still kept me awake. I knew I'd be so tired tomorrow I'd probably sleep right through my first class.

I waited for five more minutes, and then I threw my pillow on the floor and sat bolt upright.

"Do you *really* want to know what Roger said about you?" I asked. "Do you?"

When she didn't answer, I went on. "He said it's a shame that you use so much makeup when you are so much prettier without it. And he said it's too bad you don't show any respect for older people. And now that you know, will you please be quiet and let me get some sleep?"

I groped around in the dark for my pillow. All I could feel was Arthur's hairy body. He was snoring away as usual. Finally I gave up and settled down without it. There was no sound from Vicki's end of the room. I waited for her to say something; but she didn't, and after a while I heard her crawl back under blankets. Then there was only silence.

I was already regretting my outburst. I really hadn't intended to tell her. But then again, if I didn't tell her the truth, she'd mope about Roger forever. Maybe now she'd stop dreaming about him and stick to her old boyfriends instead.

Even though I was dead tired, it took awhile for me to fall asleep. With my luck the baby would probably wake me up at six again. Or even earlier.

Chapter 16

Mr. Campbell gave me an A− on my TES project, which I thought was nice of him. I still thought it was a flop, and I was relieved that it was all over and done with. It'll probably be years before I agreed to do another project.

Mom let me change Jonathan's diaper this morning. I told her Jonathan recognizes me now because he laughed and gurgled when I was cleaning him up.

"He is always happy when he gets a dry diaper on," she said. "It doesn't matter to him who is changing it."

I poked him gently in the stomach, and he smiled again. "Look," I said. "He smiles like that only when I'm here."

"He smiles at everybody. He's a very happy little boy." She picked him up. "Except when he is hungry, of course."

"Don't you ever get tired of feeding him?" I asked. "I mean, don't you think he should be on the bottle soon? Then I could help and you'd have time to do other things."

Mom is breast-feeding Jonathan now, and she plans to do that until she goes back to work again; that will be in a couple of months. Even then she'll probably work only part time to begin with.

"Of course, I don't get tired of it," Mom said reproachfully. "I'd do it forever if I didn't have to go back to work."

"Forever?" I started giggling. "You mean even when he starts school?" I could see it already. The other kids would bring their lunch boxes. Jonathan would bring Mom. I giggled again.

Mom gave me a withering look. "School?" she said. "Sometimes, Karen, your sense of humor is really warped."

Before I left, I gave Jonathan a big kiss. He really is the most beautiful baby I have ever seen.

Mom gets up at five-thirty now and feeds the baby, and then she goes jogging until seven. She has been trying to get Dad to go with her, but so far she hasn't had any luck.

Mom explained to me that she is a morning person and Dad is a night person: that is why she likes to get up early and he doesn't.

"Did you know that before you married?" I asked interestedly.

"No, I didn't."

"Shouldn't a morning person marry another morning person? I mean, you're supposed to like the same things, aren't you?"

Mom pondered that for a moment. "Not necessarily,"

she said. "Of course, you should agree about some things. Things that are really important."

"Like what?"

"Oh, like where you want to live. And whether you should have children or not. Things like that."

"What if you have children and then you find out that you'd really be happier without them?"

Mom laughed. "I guess then it's too late. You can't say you want them today and then tomorrow you don't. Once they are there, you're stuck with them."

"Until they leave home."

"Until they leave home. But usually that doesn't happen until they are at least eighteen."

"Of course, it helps if you live in Alabama," I said.

Mom looked puzzled. "It does?"

"Sure. Down there you can get married when you're fourteen. Miss Stevens told us. Just imagine," I said dreamily. "Vicki could already be married. And in a year it would be my turn."

Mom went into helpless laughter. "I'll remember that when things get tough. Maybe Dad will want to move soon."

Next week Jonathan will be getting formula for his two o'clock feeding. Dad is going to get up and give him his bottle every other night so Mom can get some uninterrupted sleep. I asked Dad if he had done that when Ryan was a baby, and he said no, he hadn't.

"But that's why I'm looking forward to it now."

"I don't see how anybody can look forward to getting up at two in the morning," I said. "I bet you'll change your mind after a few nights."

Dad looked hurt. "Really, Karen. If your mother can do it, I should be able to. It's not such a big deal after all."

"Just remember," I warned. "You're ten years older

100

than she is. At your age you have to be careful." Dad will be forty next summer; that means he's middle-aged.

Dad laughed. "I'm still strong enough to hold one baby and one bottle."

"Just don't walk around," I said. "Sit down while you feed him. You might go back to sleep and drop him, you know."

Dad looked thoughtful. "You might be right," he said. "Maybe it's too risky. And we don't want anything to happen to Jonathan, do we?"

"Exactly," I said. "I'm glad you understand."

"Oh, I do. I really do." He sounded very serious. "I'll take your advice and forget about feeding Jonathan. Just to be on the safe side."

"Good," I said.

"But since I still would like your mother to get a good night's sleep, I'll suggest to her that you take over the two o'clock feeding instead. After all, you are a very responsible person."

Me and my big mouth. "You're the one who promised to do it," I reminded him. "She's counting on you. Besides, if I don't get enough sleep, I'll sleep in class, and then I'll flunk. You don't want me to flunk, do you?"

Dad tried very hard not to laugh. "Of course not. I wouldn't dream of it." He coughed. "Thanks anyway for all your advice. I don't know what I'd do without it."

"You're welcome," I said.

Chapter 17

After I had told Vicki what Roger had said about her, she didn't talk to me for two whole days. I did my best best to stay out of her way. I still felt bad for telling, but then I figured she had practically forced me to, so I shouldn't have to feel guilty about it.

Today she was back to normal again. I noticed the last couple of days that she hadn't been smearing on all that war paint at school the way she used to. All she used this morning was blusher and lip gloss.

I know Vicki is hoping Roger will ask her to the dance, but she's not the only one. All the girls in high school are crazy about him.

Of course, I think Vicki is prettier than everybody else. Especially now without all the makeup. Vicki has a photo of her mother on her dresser. She was really beautiful, and Vicki looks a lot like her.

Since it was Friday, I decided to get my room cleaned before dinner just in case Mom and Dad decided to go into town. Dad said this morning he might get tickets for a play, and Mom said that if he did, I could be in charge of Jonathan while they were gone.

Vicki was lying on the floor, listening to records. I straightened up my drawers really quickly, and then I went downstairs for the vacuum cleaner. When I came back up, Vicki was standing looking at her closet.

To make up for what I did the other night, I said, "If you're going to clean your side of the room now, I'll wait and vacuum the whole floor after you're done."

I don't think she even heard me. She just kept staring at the mess and biting on her fingernails.

Then suddenly she spoke up.

"Do you want to help me go through my clothes? There's probably a lot of stuff that might fit you."

She didn't have to ask me twice. I love getting new clothes. Pretty soon we were busy digging through her closet and drawers. By dinnertime we weren't even half-way done.

"What on earth are you two doing up there?" Mom asked as we sat down at the table. "I haven't heard that much squealing and giggling in ages."

I helped myself to some soup. "We have been trying on clothes," I explained. "Vicki is cleaning out her closet."

Grandma raised her eyes to the ceiling and said, "Hallelujah. Miracles still happen."

"I'm just trying to weed out the things that are too small for me," Vicki said, annoyed.

I went into a hysterical giggle, and Dad stared disapprovingly at me. I covered my mouth with the napkin and tried to control myself. "We have already found two shirts and a skirt that are too small even for me," I said. "They might fit Meghan next year."

"I guess that tells us how long they have been there," Grandma commented. "When was the last time you went through your clothes, Vicki?"

Vicki took a dab of butter that was so small you could hardly see it and spread it on her roll. She is always counting calories. "I can't remember," she said offhandedly. "Not too long ago."

"She means she did it within the last five years," Marcus explained. "She might do it again when she gets married."

I almost choked on my soup. "What do you think about us moving to Alabama, Dad?" I asked.

Everybody but Mom stared blankly at me.

"It's supposed to be a beautiful state," I continued. "The laws are very liberal, too."

"You don't say." Mom tried to remain serious.

Dad looked lost. "I'm not sure what you are alluding to," he said. "What laws are you talking about? I hope you're not in trouble."

Marcus snickered. "She's talking about the legal age for drinking." he said. "What is it in Alabama? Fifteen?"

I stared coldly at him. "I was referring to the fact that you can get married down there when you're fourteen. Maybe if we lived there, I wouldn't have to put up with you anymore."

Dad rose from the table. "Well, well" he said. "That sounds interesting. I'll have to look into that. Maybe some of you could move down there."

When we finally were done with the closet, there was so much empty space I could hardly believe it. Neither could Vicki. Immediately she started making a list of the new clothes she would need to fill it up again. I bet that when Mom and Dad get to see the list, they'll wish Vicki hadn't bothered to clean her closet in the first place.

While Mom and Dad were at the theater, I practiced walking with the high-heeled sandals Vicki had given me. They really hurt my ankles, but they made me look a lot taller.

Jonathan was sleeping like a lamb. He is getting cuter all the time. I had the door to the nursery open just in case he should wake up. That way I could keep an eye on him while I was breaking in my sandals.

The Millers have invited us to an open house next week, and I want to be able to wear them. Mom probably will think the heels are too high for me. That's why I might not show them to her until we are ready to leave. If I'm lucky, she won't even notice.

If she says something, I can tell her that Jenny borrowed my old sandals. She wouldn't want me to wear sneakers with my dress. At least I hope she wouldn't. When it comes to grown-ups, you can never be sure of anything.

Chapter 18

Without forewarning winter came. Saturday morning Ryan came running up the stairs, yelling at the top of his lungs. "It's snowing. Wake up, you guys. Look outside. It's snowing." He ran around, banging on everybody's door.

Yawning, I moved the curtain aside and looked out. There were at least three inches of snow on the ground, and it was still falling in large, soft flakes. Quickly I got dressed and ran downstairs. Ryan was already getting ready to go outside.

"Hurry up," he said impatiently. "Let's get the sleds out."

At nine Jenny and Jeremy came over, and we had a

snowball fight. Pretty soon we were soaked and had to go inside. We watched cartoons while our coats and mittens were running in the dryer. Mom had gone to the basement to find our snow boots and snow pants. I knew, of course, that my boots from last year would be too small since I've grown a lot since then.

As soon as our clothes were dry, we went back outside. Mom let me borrow her boots.

Now it was snowing so heavily you could hardly see anything. Maybe there wouldn't be any school on Monday if this kept up.

Ryan and Meghan and Jeremy had started building a snow fort behind the house, so Jenny and I took one of the sleds and walked down the road to her place. Her dad was plowing their driveway with the tractor. He waved at us as he drove past.

After about an hour of pulling the sled up the hill and sledding down again, we were hot and sweaty. "Let's go inside and have a drink," Jenny suggested. "Besides, I have to go to the bathroom."

When we came into the Reddingers' kitchen, Jenny's mom was on the phone. We took a can of soda each from the fridge and continued into the living room.

"Karen, dear." Mrs. Reddinger was coming behind us. "That was Marcus on the phone. You are supposed to go home. Right away."

"Oh, no," I said in dismay. "How come? It's only eleven. Did he say what for?"

Mrs. Reddinger's face was serious. "It's your grandmother," she said. "She had a heart attack and has been taken to the hospital. Your parents and Vicki went with her in the ambulance. You're supposed to go home and help take care of the baby."

I stared at her in stunned disbelief. "Heart attack?" I

said. "But Grandma was fine when I left. I mean, I talked to her. She didn't—" A terrible thought struck me. "She isn't dead, is she?"

"Of course not." Mrs. Reddinger put a reassuring arm around me. "Nevertheless, dear, heart attacks can be rather serious sometimes." She changed the subject. "Now, why don't you get your coat and I'll have my husband drive us over with the tractor?"

She went ahead of me out into the hall. "I told your brother I'd come along. Just in case I can be of some help." She looked over her shoulder at Jenny. "Make lunch, will you, honey? Cheese sandwiches. And there is soup left from yesterday. I'll be back as soon as I can."

I don't remember how we got home, but as soon as we drove up in the yard, Marcus came out. He looked scared. We all went inside, and Mrs. Reddinger checked on Jonathan.

Marcus was standing in the doorway while she was changing his diaper. "I hope Grandma will be okay," he said nervously. "She just fell in the kitchen, and her lips were all blue—"

Mrs. Reddinger didn't let him finish. "I'm sure she'll come through with flying colors," she said firmly. She picked Jonathan up and carried him into the living room. Ryan and Meghan were playing a game. "In any case," she continued, "we'll call the hospital in half an hour if we haven't heard anything. She hasn't had a heart attack before, has she?"

Marcus shook his head. "I don't think so." He seemed more like himself now when somebody else was in charge. I hadn't even taken my boots off, and now I noticed the snow melting on the carpet. I shivered, even though it was warm in the house.

"I think I'm going to have some hot cocoa," I said.

"Me, too." That was Meghan. "And can I have a cookie?"

We were sitting around the kitchen table when the phone rang. It was Dad. He said that Grandma was doing as well as could be expected. Jenny's mom told him she'd stay until he called again.

After we had hung up, she said, "Do you know where the formula is, Karen? He said Jonathan should have a bottle in about half an hour."

By four o'clock it had finally stopped snowing. The snowplow had gone past twice. Jenny's dad had cleared our driveway with his tractor and made a couple of turns in the yard. Marcus and I shoveled behind the house and around the garage. It helped to have something to do. I was glad Mrs. Reddinger was there, especially because of Jonathan. I wasn't that used to taking care of him yet.

A little before five Mr. and Mrs. Reddinger drove into town to pick up Mom and Vicki. They also took our pickup and left it for Dad so he could get home later on. Grandma's condition was still the same, and they were keeping her in the intensive care unit overnight.

Mrs. Olson dropped off a rice casserole. I hadn't even thought about dinner. Mom looked tired when she came home, and Vicki was unusually subdued. Nobody had any appetite except Meghan and Ryan. After I was done with the dishes, I went upstairs.

Vicki was lying on her bed, staring at the ceiling.

"Are you all right?" I asked.

"Hmmm." She didn't move.

"Did you get to see Grandma?"

"No. Dad did."

I stepped over Arthur, who was sleeping on the floor. Three of the cats were on my bed, and I had to move them over to make room for myself.

Dad came home at ten o'clock. He said Grandma was resting comfortably, but they still didn't know for sure whether she would make it.

Before I went to sleep, I heard a noise from Vicki's bed. I think she was crying.

Chapter 19

It was another couple of days before we knew for sure that Grandma would be okay again. The doctors said that if her condition continued to improve, she'd be able to come home by the end of the week.

"But after this Grandma will have to take it very easy," Dad said. "No more heavy work and no lifting."

"I'm afraid it's been my fault that she has worked too hard lately," Mom said guiltily.

"I think we all are to blame." Dad looked around at all of us. "From now on we'll just have to learn to manage without Grandma."

Vicki was quieter than usual, and I noticed that she helped around the house without being asked. I knew I should be doing that, too, but by the time I'd had dinner and done my homework it was almost bedtime.

Meghan missed Grandma, and she started following Mom around, demanding her attention.

Vicki was actually doing some studying, and she had stopped experimenting with her hair; that meant the rest of us were able to get into the bathroom without waiting forever.

My hair was getting long, and pretty soon I'd need another perm. In the meantime, I used my electric curlers almost every night.

After I got into my pajamas, I sat down cross-legged on the floor to do my math. Vicki was immersed in her homework.

"Has Roger asked you to the dance yet?" I asked.

She didn't even look up. "Not yet," she said complacently. "But he will."

"How do you know?"

She shrugged. "I just know."

I changed the subject. "Have you told Mom yet about all the new clothes you want?"

Vicki straightened up and put her pen down. Her face was serious.

"No, she said at last. "I don't think right now is a good time." She studied her fingernails. She didn't even have any polish on. Usually they are dark red. "I've done a lot of thinking since Grandma got sick.

"Roger was right, you know. I haven't been very nice to Grandma. And I was afraid she would die before I had a chance to tell her how much I love her." She swallowed.

"I don't know if this makes any sense to you, but I was really glad when Dad decided to get married again. Only at the same time I resented it. I guess I was jealous and I was mad because of you and Meghan. He could have found somebody who didn't have children."

I remembered my own reaction when Mom told me that she was getting married. I hadn't liked the idea of him having three kids either.

"And because I was angry at everybody, I took it out mostly on you and Grandma. I didn't even think of how hard it must have been for her. She never complained.

"Meghan wasn't really any problem, but I got so tired of hearing how smart you were and what a good cook you were and how neat you kept your room and . . . frankly, I couldn't stand you."

I suddenly remembered my conversation with Dad. "Did you know that Dad told me you have inherited his scientific brain, only you're not using it?"

"He said that?" Vicki sounded pleased. Then she sighed. "I've really made a mess of things, haven't I?"

I giggled. "At least your closet is cleaned out," I said.

"Hmmm." She was silent for a while. "I won't ever let it get that bad again. Honest." She grinned. "Remember when you first moved here and you showed me how your clothes were organized by color?"

I nodded.

"Well, I thought you were such a showoff, I ran upstairs and pulled all the clothes out of my dresser drawers and threw them on the floor. They lay there for a week."

I stretched out on my stomach. Two of my curlers fell on the floor, and I gave them to the cats to play with.

"The first time I saw you after I knew who you were I thought you looked like a fashion model," I said. "And after I came here, I envied you your nose."

"My *nose*? What on earth for?"

"Promise you won't tell if I tell you why?"

"I promise."

"Well," I confessed, "I've always been afraid that I

might need glasses someday because I always read a lot. Only if I did, I won't be able to wear them. The glasses, I mean."

"Why not?" Vicki said, puzzled.

I pointed at my nose. "Because of this. My nose doesn't have any bridge. There isn't anything there for the glasses to rest on."

Vicki's mouth fell open, and she burst into laughter.

"It's not funny," I said crossly. "You're lucky you're not Korean. Meghan's nose is just like mine. On her it looks cute, but when you get to be as old as I am, it's embarrassing."

Vicki restrained herself. "Sorry," she said. "I didn't mean to make fun of you. Honestly, I think your nose looks great. It fits your face."

"Yeah, sure," I said gloomily. "Flat face and a flat nose."

"That's not true," Vicki protested. "Besides, I don't know what you are worrying about. You don't have to wear glasses if you don't want to. You can get contact lenses."

I looked at her with new respect. "Gee, thanks," I said. "I didn't even think of that."

"Besides, I know somebody who *loves* the way you look." She gave me a meaningful look.

"Who?" As if I didn't know.

"Andy. Roger told me he's crazy about you."

I felt my face turn red. "So who cares?" I said. "Besides, Andy is pretty neat, too."

"Did you know that Roger is planning on going to Harvard?"

I shook my head. "He must have pretty good grades then."

"He wants to be a lawyer." She looked dreamily out

the window. "He asked me what I plan to major in."

"What did you tell him?"

"I told him I hadn't made up mind yet, but I was leaning toward political science."

"I didn't know you were interested in that."

"Who said I was?" she said innocently. "It was the only subject I could think of right off the bat. I couldn't very well tell him I'm a D student who might not even make it to college?"

Unexpectedly she got up on her feet and positioned herself in front of the mirror. She held up her hand and looked at herself.

"I hereby solemnly swear that I will work at raising my grades to at least a B average before this school year is over. So help me God."

"Amen," I said.

We looked at each other and burst into laughter.

"Life is crazy sometimes, isn't it?" She stretched her arms up in the air while looking in the mirror. "This probably sounds terrible, but in a way I'm glad Grandma had her heart attack. I mean, I'm sorry she got sick, but I'm glad something happened to shake me up. Too bad it had to be something that serious." She sat down on the bed again. "Suddenly I realized how much I have to be thankful for. And how I've been wasting my time . . . "

"On romance books."

She smiled. "That, too. Maybe I'll give them to you."

"Thanks, but no, thanks."

Somebody banged on the door. It was Marcus. "Vicki. Telephone."

"Who is it?"

"I think it's Roger."

Vicki took off like a shot. When she was by the door, I said, "When you're done, tell Roger I want to talk to

Andy." I added hastily, "It's about our English test."

Vicki raised her eyebrows. "Really?" She went out and slammed the door.

I went over to the mirror and studied my profile. Maybe my nose didn't look that bad after all.

Chapter 20

"Karen, will you pour the milk for me?" Meghan was pulling at my pajama sleeve.

"In a second," I said without taking my eyes off the television. "I want to see how this ends." I was watching a Hitchcock movie, and the murderer was stalking his next unsuspecting victim.

Meghan curled up beside me on the couch. "When is Grandma coming home?"

"Monday." The murderer raised his knife, ready to plunge it into the back of the girl. Suddenly the door was kicked in and two policemen were standing there. . . .

"Will you play with me after breakfast?"

I got up and stretched. "I don't have time. I have to go to a 4-H meeting at ten. Why don't you play with Ryan?"

Meghan sniffed and wiped her nose with her sleeve. "He's still sleeping."

Looking at her bare feet, I said, "Why don't you wear your slippers? No wonder you have a runny nose."

She wiggled her toes. "I can't find them."

"Mom will help you."

Meghan wiped her nose again. "She's busy with the baby." Her face was unhappy. "How come she always has time for him and never for me?"

"Because he's little, that's why. He can't take care of himself."

"I want Grandma to come home."

I sighed. "I know," I said. One week without Grandma, and already the household was falling apart.

The front door slammed, and I heard Dad's voice. "Marcus, I'm ready to leave. Hurry up."

"Coming." Marcus came running down the stairs.

"Dad," I said, "who's going to take me to 4-H? I have to be there at ten."

Dad rubbed his chin. "You could come with me, except"—he glanced at my pajamas and robe—"you're not even dressed. And I'm afraid I don't have time to wait. I'm already running late. Marcus," he hollered again, "I'm leaving."

"He's in the kitchen," I said. "What time are you coming back?"

"Not until two o'clock."

Mom was making her bed, and Jonathan was lying on a blanket on the floor, waving his arms. "Hello there, superbaby," I said. "Are you being a good boy?"

Jonathan gurgled happily, and Mom said, "Thank goodness he's feeling better. He kept me up most of the night. I was beginning to think he was coming down with something."

"Did you know we're out of eggs?" I said. "And there is hardly any bread left?"

Mom picked up the baby and started to feed him. "I know, Karen." She sounded tired. "I haven't been to the store all week. As soon as Dad gets home with the truck, I'll drive into the supermarket."

"What about me?" I complained. "I need a ride into town in half an hour."

"Isn't Jenny going?"

"I guess so."

"Well," Mom said reasonably, "call and tell her there is nobody here to drive you."

I headed for the kitchen.

"And wake Vicki, will you? There are tons of laundry waiting to be folded."

Jenny's oldest brother drove us to town. When I came home, Vicki had gone skiing with Roger. Ryan was doing dishes, and Meghan was hanging onto Mom while she was tucking Jonathan in.

"Are we cleaning house today?" I asked.

Mom stifled a yawn. She really looked beat. "As soon as the others are back." She looked at Jonathan. He was already asleep.

We tiptoed out of the nursery, and Mom said, "I'm going to fix dinner, and you can heat it up later if I'm not back from the store yet." She ruffled Meghan's hair. "And you go upstairs and take a nap."

"I'm not tired," Meghan said stubbornly. "I want you to read me a story."

"Not right now," Mom said wearily. "Be a good girl and go lie down."

Meghan started whining. "I don't want to," she said. "Grandma always reads me a story first."

When I came into the kitchen, Ryan was blowing bubbles with the dish soap. He hadn't even started the dishes. I thought I'd better leave before Mom found out.

By the time Mom left for the supermarket it was almost four o'clock. Dad was late, and she needed the truck. We haven't been able to use the car since the snow came because it still doesn't have any snow tires.

Jonathan had been cranky all afternoon, and when Mom left, Vicki was carrying him around. She couldn't put him down because every time she did he started crying.

I served dinner, and then I helped Meghan get her dollhouse set up. She really had been a pest all day. Ryan had Jeremy over, and they didn't want any girls hanging around.

It was Vicki's turn to do the dishes, but she was still busy with the baby, so everything was stacked in the sink when Mom came back.

When she called from downstairs, I was lying on my bed, reading a magazine.

"K-a-r-e-n."

"I'm up here," I called back.

A moment later Mom stood in the doorway. "Would you mind doing the dishes? I have to put away the groceries."

I covered my face with the magazine. "Do I have to?" I groaned. "It's not my turn."

"I know. But Vicki is giving Jonathan his bath." She rubbed her cheek with her forefinger. She always does that when she is very tired. I just remembered she'd been up most of the night.

"All right." Reluctantly I got on my feet. "But that means that Vicki has to take my turn next time."

When we came to the kitchen, I asked, "Did you get a zipper for my jeans?"

Mom looked guilty. "I'm afraid I forgot. I'll get it Monday for sure."

I squeezed the soap bottle. It made a weird noise. There were only about five drops left. "Are we going to the Millers' tomorrow?"

Mom's face went blank. "Millers'? Oh, that's right. Tomorrow is their open house." She thought for a moment. "I don't think I will, but you all can go with Dad."

I turned on the water. This was even better. If Mom wasn't going, I wouldn't have to worry about her seeing my new sandals. Dad never notices what anybody wears.

After I was done with the dishes, I went into the family room to watch television. Ryan and Jeremy were playing Life. Meghan's Barbie doll stuff was all over the couch, and I had to step over a half-finished puzzle right by the door. Somebody must have been looking for something in the mending basket because most of its contents had been pulled out.

The drapes were moving, and I could see Arthur's tail sticking out from behind them. He was trying not to be in the way as usual. His dog bones were scattered around the floor.

Usually I like Saturday nights because the whole house is neat and clean. Today it looked worse than ever. I turned around and went back upstairs.

Chapter 21

When we arrived at the Millers', there were already a lot of people there. Some of them I knew, like the Reddingers and our other neighbors and a couple of families from town.

Mom had made me eat a big lunch at home so I wouldn't pig out and disgrace myself. Because of that, I wasn't very hungry, but I still managed to sample just about everything they had. They even had smoked salmon. I love smoked salmon.

Andy took me downstairs to the game room to show me his dad's gun collection. I still wasn't used to my heels, and I almost fell flat on my face going down. Fortunately Andy didn't notice.

When we first came, Roger was talking to Paula Carson. She's a senior and one of the most popular girls at school. I nudged Vicki and told her to go and grab Roger, but Vicki just shook her head.

"If he wants to talk to me, he can come over to where I

am," she said calmly. "He saw us coming."

"You mean, you're going to let Paula monopolize him just like that?" I said. "What's the matter with you?"

But Vicki just shrugged and went over to Mrs. Miller, who was standing by the window. I can't get over how much Vicki has changed in just a week. All of a sudden she has started to act like a grown-up.

We stayed only about an hour, and then Dad rounded us up so we could go home again.

Vicki didn't say a word on the way home, and I didn't bother her because I thought maybe she was in a bad mood.

As soon as we came into our room to change clothes, I said, "How did it go?"

Vicki unexpectedly turned around and gave me a big hug. "Oh, Karen!" she exclaimed. "He asked me to the dance." Her eyes were shining. I had never seen her so happy before.

Excitedly I hugged her back. "Gee," I said. "that's great. I bet you can't wait until next week."

Vicki and I had been living in the same house for more than a year, but I think that right now for the first time I truly felt that she was my sister. It was a good feeling. In the past there had been periods when we were getting along, I had sometimes felt she was my friend, but we had never been close the way sisters should be.

"What are you going to wear?" I asked.

"Hmmmm." She looked thoughtful. "If I can't have a new dress, I'll wear my old green one." She sat down on her bed and started putting on her sweater. "Maybe Mom will let me buy new shoes."

It was a relief to get back into jeans again. I like dressing up but not for very long. Besides, my ankles were hurting from those high heels.

"I wish I could start going to dances," I said enviously. "Twelve and a half is a terrible age. Not to mention that it seems to last forever."

Vicki smiled sympathetically. "Enjoy it while it lasts," she said. "The older you get, the more problems you have. Believe me, I know."

"Some of the girls in my class are already dating," I pointed out. "I wish Mom wouldn't be so strict."

After dinner it started snowing again. Later in the evening the wind increased, and the storm that had been forecast hit us in the early morning. If the plows had been out at all during the night, it certainly didn't show. At seven, when I woke up and looked outside, you couldn't even see where the country road was. It was completely drifted over.

Dad had already listened to the local news, and he came up and told us that the school was closed.

At nine, when it finally stopped snowing, we all went outside and started shoveling, but it was almost noon before the first snowplow came through.

We made our own sandwiches for lunch. Jonathan had a slight fever and refused to go to sleep, so Mom carried him around while she made some attempt to pick up the mess around the house. The breakfast dishes were still not done, and the hall floor was so littered with wet boots and coats and mittens that you could hardly see it.

Dad came in stamping his feet to get the snow off. He had been clearing the garage roof.

"Brr," he said. "It's getting colder out there. I don't remember ever having such weather in November before."

"Are you bringing Grandma home today?" I asked.

Dad shook his head. "I called the hospital this morning and told them I'd be in tomorrow. Provided we don't get any more snow dumped on us today," he added. "By the way, where is Marcus? I need help to put the chains on the pickup."

He looked at the mess on the floor. "How about putting some of this stuff away?" he said irritably. "A person can't even walk through here anymore."

"It's all wet," I said. "Where am I supposed to put it?"

"How about in the dryer?"

"Mom is drying diapers."

Dad frowned. "Well, at least get it off the floor." I carried the whole mess into the utility room, where I dumped it on the floor. There wasn't any other place because of all the laundry that was piled everywhere.

Afterward I went to the basement to try to find Mom's ski boots. She said I could borrow them until I got a pair that fitted me. I'd still have to use the skis I had last year, even though they were on the short side.

Of course, the boots weren't where they were supposed to be. I searched the closet and the cabinets, and I was in the middle of going through the stuff in the big old wardrobe when Ryan came down the stairs.

"Dad says for you to come up," he said.

I pulled out the bottom drawer. "As soon as I've found what I'm looking for," I said.

"He said right now."

"What does he want?"

Ryan shrugged. "I don't know. He just wants everybody to come to the living room. Right now," he repeated.

When I came into the living room, everybody else was there. Dad was standing over by the fireplace, looking grim. I was suddenly struck by a thought.

"Grandma isn't worse, is she?" I said out loud.

Dad's face relaxed. "No, of course not," he said. "That's not what I want to talk to you about." He folded his arms and looked around. "However, it's because of what happened to Grandma that we need to have this family conference."

We all looked at him.

"I don't know if you have noticed, but things haven't been the same since Grandma went to the hospital," he continued. "Mom has a lot more work to do besides having the baby to take care of. I gather that you kids have done your chores more or less in time, but there hasn't been any effort to pitch in and do anything beyond that. Am I right?"

Mom, who was sitting with Meghan in her lap, said loyally, "They usually do help when I ask them to. But I think we need to assign everybody a few more chores."

I raised my hand. "I'll do some of the cooking," I volunteered, "if somebody else does the dishes."

"Hah!" Marcus exclaimed. "How come you can't do them yourself? Cooking is the fun part. Maybe I'll cook and you can do the dishes."

"You don't even know how to cook," Vicki said scornfully.

Marcus turned to her. "I do, too. I can cook lots of different things."

Now Mom got into the conversation. "Why don't you three take turns fixing dinner one day a week? That way I'll have three days that I don't have to do it, and maybe I can get some other things done instead."

Vicki, Marcus, and I looked at each other. "That's fine with me," Vicki said.

"And we'll do our own dishes," I said.

"Can we fix anything we want?" Marcus asked.

"Well . . . " Mom hesitated. "Within reason. Maybe

we can make up a weekly menu. That way there won't be any arguments, and we can make sure we have whatever is needed ahead of time."

"What about me?" Meghan said forlornly. "I want to cook, too."

Dad went over and sat down beside Mom's chair. "Of course, honey," he said. "You and I will make breakfast every Monday morning. I couldn't do it by myself."

"Oh, my," Mom said. "If only Ryan would take charge of the rest of the meals, I guess I won't ever have to set foot in the kitchen myself. What more could a mother ask for?"

We all laughed, except Ryan, who said. "I'm not going to fix any crummy meals. I'd rather fold the laundry."

"Well," Mom said, "you can take turns doing that."

"I hate folding laundry," Marcus muttered.

"I'll do it all the time," Ryan said. "Honest, I will." He looked at Mom. "Can I?"

"You mean, you want to do the laundry all the time?" Ryan nodded. "I want to."

Mom and Dad both looked surprised, but Dad said, "It's all right with me. In fact, I don't mind if Arthur does the laundry as long as I don't have to do it."

Then Dad gave us the big news. "Guess what?" he said. "We're going to install another bathroom in the basement. No tub, just a shower."

"Yippee," Ryan shouted. "Another bathroom."

Even Mom looked surprised. "You really mean that?" she said. "How come you didn't tell me?"

Dad looked smug. "Because I didn't think of it until this morning," he said. "I had a couple of the students ask me the other day whether I knew of any temporary work they could do, and this morning I suddenly had the brilliant idea to let them put in another bathroom. I don't have time myself, and it's too costly to hire a professional to do it." He paused and winked at Vicki. "It's amazing what you have time to think about when you are waiting to get into the bathroom."

Vicki's face turned pink, and she said, "I didn't think I was in there that long."

Dad grinned. "Just kidding," he said. "But there is no doubt that we can use another bathroom."

When our family conference was over, I got the job of printing our new schedule of chores on a poster board and taping it to the side of the refrigerator. We had covered just about everything that needed to be done in the house, and most of the chores would be rotated, with one person doing each one a week at a time.

After dinner we all pitched in to clean the whole house so at least we could start our new chores without having to break our backs.

After we had gone to bed, Vicki said suddenly, "Isn't this exactly what you were trying to get us to do with your project?"

I sat up. "Yeah," I said slowly. "It is. But nobody listened to me." I hadn't thought of that myself. But Vicki was right. This was what should have happened back then. Only it didn't.

"I guess if Grandma hadn't gotten sick, we still wouldn't have changed anything." Vicki's voice was thoughtful. "Just like I wouldn't have changed."

I hugged my knees in the dark. "You also wanted to change because of Roger," I said. "Not only because of Grandma."

Vicki was silent. Then I heard her turn in her bed. "I guess you are right," she said in a muffled voice. "Good night. I hope we have school tomorrow."

I'm sure we will," I said. "It hasn't snowed any more."

In a way I felt resentful that my family finally was getting organized. They were doing it without any help from me. Why couldn't they have cooperated when I wanted them to shape up? Somehow it wasn't fair. Why couldn't it have happened while I was still doing my project? At least then I could have taken some credit for it.

But maybe Mr. Campbell would let me add to my report. I'd ask him tomorrow.

Chapter 22

Since I wasn't in Mr. Campbell's class on Tuesdays anymore, I stopped him when he was leaving the cafeteria. Mrs. Sanders was with him, so all I asked was if I could add a couple of pages to my report.

"Certainly," he said. "That's fine with me." He thought for a moment. "In fact, why don't you show your TES project at the science fair next month? I think it has a good chance of winning."

I had forgotten all about the science fair. Last year I won second prize for my soap project. I had tested different brands of bar soap and compared their cleaning performance.

On the way home I was thinking about what else I could do with my TES to get it ready for the fair. It seemed I had barely gotten on the bus before we were home.

Grandma was lying on the sofa in the living room. She looked fine except I think she had lost some weight. We all were glad to see her, especially Meghan. She had probably missed her more than anybody else.

I wrote three new pages to add to my report. It explained all about Roger and Grandma's illness and how it got the whole family motivated.

It took me two hours to type it, and when I was done, I thought it was pretty good. Tomorrow I'd stay after school and go the library and do some research. I wanted to get some information about time efficiency studies in general and whatever else I could find.

Vicki was in charge of dinner. She had made spaghetti. For dessert we had apple cobbler, which was really good.

"I didn't know you were such a good cook," I said. "This is delicious."

Vicki beamed at me. It was hard to believe that only a month ago she had torn down my sign from her door and got chewed out by Dad.

"Just wait until Monday," Meghan said importantly.

"What's happening on Monday?" Grandma wanted to know.

Meghan slid down from her chair and took the chart off the refrigerator. "Here," she said, handing it to Grandma. "Dad and I are making breakfast on Mondays."

Grandma studied the chart carefully. "Well, well," she said finally. "This looks like something we should have had a long time ago." She patted Meghan's head. "I can't wait until Monday. What are we going to have?"

"Everything," Meghan declared. "Eggs and sausage and bacon and pancakes and waffles and oatmeal and corn flakes and—"

"Wait a minute . . . wait a minute." Dad looked horrified. "It's supposed to be a breakfast, not a banquet. I was thinking of cereal and toast and juice," he continued. "Something simple."

"Dad doesn't know how to cook, does he?" Meghan said to Grandma.

Grandma nodded. "That's what it sounds like, all right."

"How come you didn't teach him?"

"Oh, I tried," Grandma reassured her. "Lots of times." She took a bite from her roll. "He's a very slow learner."

"Well, thanks a lot," Dad said dryly. "As a matter of fact, I make very good pancakes."

"What a coincidence." Mom looked pleased. "That's what is on the menu for Monday. Pancakes and bacon."

"Gee, Dad," Meghan said. "Aren't we lucky?"

Dad didn't look very enthusiastic when he said, "Yeah. How lucky can you be?"

I gave the new pages to Mr. Campbell on Thursday. He read them while I was doing my math packet on the computer.

When he was done, he said, "I think this is excellent. I'm going to show it to Mr. Dressler, if you don't mind." Mr. Dressler is the science teacher for the high school.

"Sure," I said. "Do you really think it has a chance at the fair?"

"Absolutely. Of course, you have to type this over. There are a couple of mistakes. Make it really neat."

"I know," I said. "Maybe I'll borrow Mom's type-writer. Mine jumps."

When I told Mom about the science fair, she said, "And where are the winners going this year?"

"To Portland to compete with the junior high schools there." Last year we got to go to Walla Walla, which is a very small town. I didn't even get an honorable mention for my soap project. I would much rather go to Portland. I like big cities. Not to live in but to visit.

Grandmother called to see how everbody, especially Jonathan and Grandma, was doing. I was the last one who got to talk to her.

"When are you coming?" I asked.

"Next Wednesday."

"Great." Then I added cautiously, "How is your boyfriend?"

"He's fine, thank you. How is yours?"

I giggled and felt my face turn red. I was glad she couldn't see me. "Fine. And you should see Vicki's new date. He's a dream. He's taking her to the high school dance. And he's going to be a lawyer."

"Good. I hope she'll marry him. Every family should have a lawyer."

"Why?"

"Oh, just in case you need one. Lawyers are very expensive, you know. It helps to have one right in the family."

The next day I asked Larry Porter what his entry was going to be. He won first prize last year.

"I'm building a hydro plant," he said. "It's taking forever."

I thought that sounded impressive. The judges usually like things that look like they took a long time to make.

When I came home, I counted my money. I had exactly seventeen dollars and three cents. Most of it came from the sale of my old bike. Usually I spend my allowance as fast as I get it.

If I won at the fair, it would mean I'd be going to Portland the second week in December. That meant that I could do some of my Christmas shopping there. We usually get a few hours to look around before heading home again.

From now on I'd better start saving my allowance. The trouble with money is that it's so hard to earn and so easy to spend. At least for me.

Chapter 23

I spent most of the evening working on my report. It was seven pages long, and twice I had to do a page over because I had skipped something. It made me so mad I almost chucked the whole thing.

I was still using my own typewriter. Mom lent me hers, but I made too many mistakes with it. I don't see how anyone can say that electric typewriters are time-saving.

I had got only as far as page four when Dad came home. He was carrying a big box.

"Karen, open the door to the den, will you?"

I did, and he put the box on his desk. Then he went back out and brought a second box.

"What is it?" I asked. "Anything interesting?"

Dad took off his coat. "You might say that," he said with a satisfied smile. "It's a word processor. Just what I have been needing for a long time. The university is replacing some of their older machines, so I was able to get this one at a bargain price."

"A word processor," I said excitedly. "But that's what I need. Can I use it tonight? I have this—"

But Dad shook his head. "Oh, no," he said firmly. "This is only for me. Understand? I don't want any of you kids fiddling with it."

"But, Dad," I moaned, "I have this report for my TES project that I have to do over again so I can enter it in the science fair, and I keep on making all these mistakes and—"

Dad shook his head again. "Sorry, Karen. You have a typewriter of your own. Besides, I won't have time to get this thing set up anyway until tomorrow." He glanced at his watch. "I have to leave again soon for a lecture. Did you save any dinner for me?"

"It's in the microwave." I tried again. "Dad, after you get it hooked up, can't I just use it to type my report? I know how it works, you know. We have one at school."

I followed him to the kitchen. "It's seven pages long, and I never get it done correctly because my typewriter keeps on jumping and making spaces between the letters that shouldn't be there. Please, Dad?"

Dad sighed and patted my shoulder. "I'll think about it," he said. "How is Grandma?"

"She is fine. She's taking a nap. Oh, thanks, Dad. You're the greatest." I gave him a peck on the cheek. "Now I don't have to waste so much paper. Did you know Mr. Campbell thinks I can win first prize with my TES project?"

Dad sat down at the kitchen table. "No, I didn't. Not that it surprises me."

"And when I do, I can go to Portland. I can't wait. I bet the stores are really neat there."

"You haven't won yet."

I ignored that. I just knew I'd win. "Do you have any paid chores?" I asked. "I need to make some money."

He thought for a moment. "Not right now. Maybe next week."

I spent the next couple of days talking to the other seventh and eighth graders to find out what they were going to enter. I didn't actually see any of the projects, and a couple of kids hadn't even started theirs, but from what I heard I didn't think I had too much to worry about. Except for maybe Larry's.

Dad let me use the word processor on Saturday, and I spent the morning doing the report. It came out of the printer absolutely perfect. Dad kept on coming in to see how I was doing. I don't think he really believed I knew how to use the machine.

"Well, well," he said when I showed him the finished pages, "that should get you a few extra points for neatness, if nothing else."

"Do you want to read it?"

"Sure, honey." He took some paper clips out of his desk drawer. "Why don't you leave it here and I'll take a look at it later."

After lunch I did my chores in record time, so I could go over to Jenny's. We were going skiing.

When I came home, it was three-thirty, and the house was quiet as a tomb. I found Grandma knitting in the family room.

"Where is everybody?"

She looked up. "Oh," she said, "the little kids are

taking a nap, and I believe your mother is resting, too. Vicki and Marcus are out." She paused. "Your father is taking us out for dinner tonight. That reminds me. He was looking for you earlier."

I opened the door to the den and peeked inside. "Where are we going for dinner?" I said.

Dad was at his desk, working. "I don't know. Where do you want to go?"

"Skippers," I said promptly. "Or to a pizza place." Then I asked, "Who is going to take care of Jonathan?"

"Mrs. Olson is coming over to baby-sit."

I leafed through a copy of *Newsweek* that was lying on the desk. "Grandma said you were looking for me."

Dad sighed and drummed on the desk with his fingers. "That's right," he said. "I was. I read your report. It's very good, and I'm proud of you." Despite his words, he didn't look very happy.

"Thanks," I said. Then I waited. Obviously there was more to come.

He picked up the report and spread out the pages on the desk. "What you have written here about your sister is very relevant to your study, Karen," he said. "But how do you think Vicki will feel about it, having the whole school read about her? Don't you think it will be rather embarrassing for her?"

I stared at him with my mouth open. I hadn't even thought about that aspect.

"But the kids hardly ever bother to read the reports," I said lamely. "All they do is look at the displays and the pictures and stuff like that."

"Haven't you ever read anybody's report? Not even the ones that won?"

I had, of course. I read Larry's last year because he beat me. And I read Jenny's and a couple of others, too.

"Probably only the judges will," I said unconvincingly.

Dad gave me a you-know-better-than-that look. "Come on," he said. "All it takes is for one kid to read it and pass the word around, and everybody will know about it."

"I can take away those last three pages," I said helpfully. "I mean, the project was finished before I added those."

Dad skimmed through the report again. "That still leaves your account of Vicki locking herself up in the bathroom forever and never doing homework and living in a pigpen." He paused. "And a few other not so pleasant things."

"It's all true," I said defiantly.

"I know, honey." Dad's voice was patient. "That's not the point. Those last pages about her crush on Roger and Grandma's illness are true, too. The point is that it's really not anybody else's business to know about all these things. And as I said, to have everybody at school read about it would be rather embarrassing for Vicki."

My stomach felt funny. Why did he have to bring this up? "You mean, I can't enter my project in the fair at all?" I said.

"I didn't say that. That's entirely up to you. I'm only saying that it might hurt Vicki if you did. Try to imagine how you would feel if you were in her shoes." He handed me the report. "Here. Think about it."

I went into the kitchen and put some water on the stove for cocoa. Whenever I'm upset, I have to eat or drink something. Mom says it's a nervous habit just the way some adults automatically reach for a cigarette when they are upset.

I took my cup upstairs and sat down on the floor. I really thought Dad was overreacting. So what if everybody found out that Vicki had a crush on Roger? He was taking her to the dance, wasn't he? After that everybody would know anyway.

As for Vicki's being jealous of me, well, I had been jealous of her, too (even though this wasn't mentioned in the report). Besides, sibling rivalry was as old as the Bible.

I decided not to let it worry me. I put the tape I had borrowed from Jenny in my cassette recorder. It had the top ten country songs on it. Jenny tapes it from the radio every month.

We didn't leave until eight because Jonathan refused to go to sleep and Mom didn't want to leave until he did. He smiled and gurgled and kicked for almost an hour and didn't look the least bit tired.

"I bet he's doing it on purpose," Marcus grumbled. "I'm starving. Let's take him with us."

But Mom wouldn't even hear of that, so we all waited until Jonathan finally fell asleep. By then I had already eaten three sandwiches to tide me over.

We went to a brand-new place called the Burger Barn, which used to be an Italian restaurant. This was much nicer. They had done the whole inside over, and it looked really neat.

I had a double Barn-Burger with fries and an orange drink.

"Do we get dessert?" Ryan wondered.

We go out for dinner only every other month or so, and most of the time we don't have dessert because it gets too expensive. That's one of the drawbacks of having a large family, I guess.

Now Dad said, "I think we have reason to celebrate tonight. After all, Grandma is back with us again, and we have a new baby and . . . " He tried to think of what else there was that had happened lately.

"And Vicki is going with Roger to the dance," I said.

Vicki blushed. Then she added, "And Karen will probably win first prize at the science fair with her project."

I felt my own face turn red. Suddenly my burger seemed to grow in my mouth. I chewed and chewed, and finally I had to finish my whole drink to get it down.

"Well," Mom said loyally, "Karen certainly has worked hard enough on her project, and I think she deserves to win."

Vicki gave me a friendly nudge and said teasingly, "I bet Andy will be impressed if you do."

I mumbled something and tried to look unconcerned. It just occurred to me that Vicki didn't even know what was in that report.

Suddenly I pushed my chair back. "Excuse me," I said and headed for the rest room. Since I didn't know where it was, I ended up in the kitchen, and one of the cooks had to set me straight.

I just wanted to be alone. I wished Dad hadn't talked to me about the report. Not that I felt that I had done anything wrong. All I had written was the truth. It wasn't as if I had made anything up or even exaggerated anything.

I don't know how long I had been there when Vicki came in. "Karen, are you all right?"

"Yes," I said.

"You've been gone for ages." She sounded worried.

"I'm fine," I said. "I guess I ate too many sandwiches at home. I'll be right out."

When we came back to the table, everybody was eating ice cream sundaes.

"I didn't know what you wanted, so I ordered a vanilla for you," Dad said.

The chocolate sauce was running down the side of my glass. "That's fine," I said. "It's my favorite."

Vicki leaned over the table and said, "If you want to, you can borrow my denim skirt with the ruffles when you go to Portland. It will look perfect with your white sweater."

I swallowed and stirred my ice cream until it was all mushy. Then I looked up and smiled.

"Thanks, Vicki," I said. "That's nice of you. But I probably won't be going to Portland."

"Why not? Even if you get second prize, you'll be eligible to go."

I let the syrup drip from my spoon. "I know," I said finally. "But I've decided not to enter my project."

They all looked at me. Then Mom said, "Why on earth not?"

I looked around the table. "Well," I explained, "to tell you the truth, I'm so tired of that project that I can't stand even thinking about what kind of display I would have to make to go with it." I shrugged. "So I decided to forget about it."

Licking my spoon, I continued. "That doesn't mean I might not enter something else instead. After all, the fair isn't until three weeks from now. I have lots of time."

My eyes met Dad's, and he smiled at me. "Knowing what you are capable of, Karen, I'll say you'll probably end up walking home with a prize anyway."

All of a sudden I felt happy again. "You know something?" I said. "I might. But even if I don't win, it's okay."

Then I turned to Vicki. "Just in case," I said, "maybe I'll try your skirt on, after all, when we get home."